I0552222

Immortal Tigress

Children of the Wild, Volume 1

Prudence MacLeod

Published by Prudence MacLeod, 2024.

IMMORTAL TIGRESS

First edition. February 14, 2024.

Copyright © 2024 Prudence MacLeod.

ISBN: 978-1927478592

Written by Prudence MacLeod.

Immortal Tigress
By
Prudence MacLeod

Need

In the beginning there was need. She was only dimly aware of the world around her, a world filled with wonder, and yet fraught with danger. She was only aware of need, the need for food, for drink, safety from attack, fire for warmth and protection.

As she grew there came a new need, a need to mate, but that was not to be for she had grown too tall and strong too quickly, and thus she was shunned by the others. Eventually she became insistent and was driven away from the clan, for her sheer size and strength frightened them.

Alone and hungry, she sat beside a small tree near a stream, mourning, and trying to warm herself as she filled her empty belly with sweet grasses. Slowly she became aware of a fire in the sky. Gazing in wonder at the thing that grew steadily nearer, she was unaware of the danger stalking her. The fire from the sky hit the ground and exploded just as the great beast pounced. The beast tore at her body but was itself shredded by the exploding fireball.

Wounded and terrified, she lay beneath the body of the great cat, its life blood pouring out across her lips, while a strange glowing mist fell upon them. For a moment she drank greedily of the blood, then fainted away.

The body of the long toothed cat was still laying half across her when awareness returned, but the glowing mist was gone. The sun was up, and for some reason it disturbed her, and hurt her eyes. With a mighty heave she thrust the beast's carcass away and leaped to her feet, her wounds healed, and her great strength returned, redoubled. She wrenched a long fang with which to make a weapon, from the jaw of the cat. A moment later she found shelter from the sun among the trees. She would wait for darkness, and then she would hunt. She wanted, needed, the taste of the blood again. Now there was a stronger need than any she had ever known.

Murdered

"Vampire? Preposterous." John West met the eyes of all four of his friends and the stranger. "I don't believe a word of it."

"Please John, I know you think you love your wife, but do you really or is it just some compulsion she has laid on you?" The tall man began to sputter, but his friends hurried on. "John, how many times have you awakened to find your bed empty?"

"Ella often walks the gardens at night..."

"Yes she does," oozed the stranger in the room, a man with dark skin, cruel eyes, and a scar down the side of his face, wearing the garb of a priest. He'd said his name was Mobutu. "Don't you find that habit a bit odd, Mr. West?"

"Vampire. I just can't believe that my wife is a vampire." John West was visibly shaken and he was beginning to waver.

"Has she ever injured herself, Mr. West?" asked the priest. "If so, does she heal remarkably well? Do things that should damage the body seem to leave her unaffected? Has she aged in the fifteen years of your marriage?"

The harangue went on for hours and eventually they wore him down. John West sat, his head in his hands, shaking as he finally accepted what he was being told. "What am I going to do?"

The priest rose and passed him a vial. "This is laudanum, it will induce sleep; make certain she drinks it all. You must do this tonight before she goes for her walk. We shall be waiting for your signal. Once she's unconscious we'll come to you and deal with the rest."

"ELLA, I KNOW YOU PREFER to stay indoors during the day. Thank you so much for accompanying me."

"My skin burns too easily, Margaret, but it's a dark and cloudy day today, I'll be fine."

"Ella, what is it? You're sniffing the air like my husband's old hound."

"I thought I smelled something vile."

"Of course you did; we're not that far from London. Ah, here we are, Dr. Lawson's surgery. Just make yourself comfortable, Ella. I'm sure I won't be long."

The tall woman settled into a leather-bound chair to wait for her friend to be finished with the doctor. She tried reading, but couldn't focus on the print. Her mind wandered back over the years, thousands of years beyond anything a human could remember. She remembered the first time she had caught that scent. "Mobutu," she snarled as she ran that first meeting through her mind.

The world had been younger then and far from civilized. She had inadvertently created another like her, but not quite the same. She'd managed to gain control over the killing lust, but the other had not. Ella had stalked and killed it, later discovering that it had created more like itself, unable to control the killing lust. One by one she stalked and slew them all, all but one. Mobutu. He was the last.

She'd come upon him in a small clearing where he was tearing his victim apart slowly, trying to elicit more screams. An errant draft of wind had taken her scent to him just before she charged. He escaped. Snarling in rage at the miss, she dispatched the poor broken female he had been torturing. His scent was strong in her nostrils for she'd raked him down the face and his blood was on the ground.

She had stood snarling, testing the breeze for his scent when his voice drifted down to her from the cliff above. "I've escaped you, you murderous old hag," he'd shouted in a thick accent. "I will hunt you now. I am Mobutu; I will become your death."

Ella had hurled herself at the cliff face, but he was long gone by the time she reached the top. It was several hundred years before they met again.

Over the centuries she'd encountered him again and again. She could always tell when he was near; the sheer savagery of the slaughter would give him away. He could only control the killing lust for a short time. Then he would go on a murderous rampage. Mobutu had attacked her several times, but each time she slew him and sent the bones to Africa, hoping he would stay there.

Ella was becoming civilized and was loathe to permanently destroy the last of Tegra's line. Mobutu, on the other hand, was driven to greater madness with each defeat. Throughout much of Africa he was feared as a demon, many villages made human sacrifices to him to keep him away. It rarely worked.

Shaking off the mood, Ella laid aside the book; Margaret was returning. She rose and left the building with her friend chatting happily about her illness. Margaret continued to prattle on, but Ella was barely listening, she was on the alert for Mobutu's scent once again.

At length they arrived at Margaret's door. "Ella, thank you for accompanying me today. It's nearly dusk and I'm so afraid of walking these paths alone after dark. Will you be all right alone, or shall I send for a carriage to take you home?"

"I have no fear of the dark, Margaret," smiled Ella. "I'll be fine. You get some rest; I'll see you again tomorrow."

Ella soon left the road and took the path through the woods to her home. She'd hope to encounter Mobutu, but he was not to be seen. Laying aside her cloak and gloves, she went into the study where she found her husband nursing a glass of sherry. "Ah, there you are, Ella. Will you have a glass of sherry with me?"

"Of course, John. Are you feeling well? You look exhausted."

"Rough day at the exchange, my darling; I don't want to burden you with it." He passed her a glass then held up his own for a toast. "Here's to a better tomorrow."

They clinked glasses and drank. "This sherry tastes a little off, John."

"Nonsense, Ella, it'll do you good. You've been out in the dampness again; I don't want you to catch a chill."

Somewhat dubious, Ella drank the sherry. A few moments later she was feeling unwell. "I think I shall retire to bed, John. I do not feel well."

"Of course dear."

She made it to her bedroom and fell onto the bed. Something was terribly wrong, Ella had never been sick in all her unnaturally long life. To her horror, her limbs stopped responding to her commands, but her mind was clear. John stepped into the room to check on her. "John, send for the doctor, I can't move my arms or legs."

"What? Ella, how is it that you're still awake? You should be unconscious by now."

"John, what have you done?" Ella fought to keep the panic from her voice.

"Forgive me, Ella, but I have done this to save your immortal soul as well as countless innocent lives."

"What are you talking about? John, what have you done to me?"

Her pleading fell on deaf ears; he did not answer. Trembling, he took the lamp and signaled at the window then fled the room. A few moments later she heard voices from the bottom of the stairs. Mobutu!

"She's awake, but paralyzed. That wasn't laudanum; what did you do?" Her husband's voice was shaking with barely controlled emotion.

"Forgive me, Mr. West, I had to deceive you. She must be awake when I exorcise the demon within her," oozed Mobutu's voice. "First I must drive out the demon to save her soul, and then I must destroy the body to permanently rid the world of the vampire. I will not ask you gentlemen to observe this, but I must ask you to ignore any and all sounds that come from that room, until I call you to enter." He stopped speaking and there were footsteps on the stairs.

The door to her room opened and his maddened eyes met hers. "You won't escape me this time. I knew I would eventually succeed. There can be only one immortal, only one god." He laughed cruelly as he walked to her side and dropped a huge bag on the bed.

Her mind screamed for movement, but her body refused. She thrashed her head wildly, but all to no avail. "Struggle all you wish; I'll enjoy it. You cannot move, and you cannot transform. The effect of the drug will wear off in a few hours, but you won't be alive by then."

He pulled a long wooden stake, a hammer, and a rusty short sword from his bag. "The stake won't kill you, but I must because those gullible fools below believe that is how you kill a vampire. I will then cut off your vile head in order to truly destroy you."

"Mobutu..."

"No," he hissed as he smashed his fist into her face. "The only sounds you will make are screams. His eyes were wild, and his body trembled with the effort of controlling the rage that burned within him. Mobutu seized up the stake and, ignoring the hammer, drove the stake through her body. Unable to move or make any sound except a screaming moan of pain, Ella fought for unconsciousness, but it would not come.

"I know all about your eight little children," he slavered right at her face. "My next task will be to kill them all, one by one. I will erase all your line from the earth. I am the only god." Ella could only moan and watch in horror as he swept up the rusty blade and began hacking at her neck. As he finally severed her head, consciousness left her.

"It's done," declared Mobutu as he descended the stairs carrying her head by the hair. Two of the men below were instantly sick, losing their last meal. "You must bury the body without a marker and disguise the grave. Burn this house to the ground and declare Mrs. West perished in the fire. I will take the head far away so the vampire can never return."

"No!" John West faced Mobutu, a double-barreled shotgun in his hands. "I betrayed Ella, and she loved me. I'll take her head to our country house in the Lake District. I'll bury her there where she loved the view. That should be far enough away."

"That is unwise. You are distraught..."

"Yes I am." John leveled the gun right at Mobutu's head. "I've already committed one murder this night, priest, another will matter little. Put her down and get out of my house."

Mobutu trembled with the effort of controlling the killing lust within him, but that damned shotgun could take his head off. "As you wish, Mr. West, but I caution you all to follow my instructions. Should the vampire revive, she will go on a killing rampage. The last thing you want is a vengeful vampire on your hands."

He left the house, but slipped into the trees where he watched as the men buried the body, disguised the grave then set the house afire. John West, an ornate box under his arm, saddled his horse and rode away.

Mobutu nodded in satisfaction, tore the priest's collar from his neck, and slipped away. "Now for that accursed Saxon; I believe he's in Germany."

JOHN WEST FINALLY ARRIVED at his estate in the Lake District. Tears streamed down his face as he buried his wife's head where she could see the view.

Over the following two years he drank heavily, a fact remarked upon by the locals. After one bright full moon he vanished from the area.

A few weeks after John disappeared from the Lake District, a man staggered up to the remains of a burned out house; John West had brought Ella home. He drank deeply from a bottle then tossed the empty aside. John searched for a while, and then took out an ornate box and a small spade from his pack.

"I know this isn't the exact spot, my love, but I cannot find where they buried you. This will have to be close enough." He buried the box and disguised the place. He then pulled out a fresh bottle and drank deeply.

Down the hill he went until he reached the narrow stone bridge over the stream. Another deep draught from the bottle, then John West pulled a pistol from his pack, stuck the barrel into his mouth, and pulled the trigger.

Saxon

Europe was on the brink of war. Few folk went out at night, especially in this part of London. One man did, and he walked with confidence. A German immigrant, he said he was fleeing the war, but he went out each night, searching for something. A few hardy robbers approached him, much to their dismay. It didn't take long before the man was once again left to his own devices, almost.

It was a bitter cold night and he pulled his coat closer. He was aware of a shadow that stalked him, and he grinned in anticipation. For six long years that shadow had hunted for him, the man called the Saxon. His people had known him as Harald Eldredsson, or at least they had before he was made vampire.

He had been king of a fierce people. In his day, it was not enough to be born a king's son. One had to be a great warrior as well as an able leader. Harald Fairhair, King of Nord Saxlund had been the best. He grinned and loosened the catch on his sword cane as he caught the faint scent of his stalker: Mobutu.

It had taken a few years, but Mobutu had tracked down the Saxon. He was the next strongest, but Mobutu was older and stronger. Overflowing with confidence, and still flushed from his victory over the Old One, he had hunted the Saxon across two continents and back to London again. The Saxon was seeking his maker, of course, but he would not find her. No, but he would soon join her, Mobutu vowed.

He finally caught up with him in a narrow darkened street on the poor side of the city.

Mobutu had spent days following Harald and scouting the terrain. He knew exactly where he wanted to face his opponent. He had laid his trap well and the moment was upon him. Mobutu was already savoring the victory as he stepped out of the shadows and spoke. "Greetings, Saxon, I bring you news of your maker."

Harald didn't turn around; he just stopped and cocked his head. When he spoke his voice was deep and filled with confidence. "Mobutu, I thought the air was especially foul this evening. How long has it been, scum, since Ella last sent your useless carcass back to Africa? A century or more I'm sure. Recovered your courage, have you?"

"Bluster if you must, Saxon, but I know what you seek. You won't find her. She's dead. I killed her myself. She was so delicious, lying helpless before me. I put a stake through her heart just to hear her scream. I used a rusty blade to cut off her head, Saxon. It took several blows. She screamed at each one. Her body was burned and her head was taken out to sea and thrown overboard."

"You should stick to mad ravings, Mobutu. You're a terrible liar."

"Believe what you wish, Saxon, for the little time you have left. Prepare to die."

The big man chuckled and shrugged off his cloak. "I'll take you to Valhalla with me, Mobutu. Come to me; this is a good day to die."

Mobutu had taken on the appearance of something half man and half beast, all fang and claw. He charged with blinding speed, but Harald melted away, slashing with his sword cane. Mobutu screamed in fury and pain, blood flowing from a wound on his chest and another on his face. He turned to see that Harald had transformed into the half beast as well.

Mobutu snatched up a club from where he had hidden it and charged in again. With a howl of maddened fury, he attacked. Harald parried with the sword, but the blade snapped. He dropped the useless weapon and grabbed Mobutu's club, twisting it from his grasp. He swung a mighty blow at the madman's head, but it missed and the club shattered. It was down to hand to hand.

Mobutu fought with a fury born of insanity, ripping at his opponent with fang and claw, tearing and shredding at his flesh. Mobutu was stronger, but not by much, and Harald was a trained warrior with thousands of years of experience and practice. He fought with the cold relentlessness of the icy lands that had spawned him. Each blow was delivered with precision and power to a vital area.

They'd fought well into the night. Several buildings were damaged and so were they. Both were torn and bleeding, especially Harald, but Mobutu had several broken bones and wounds as well. They lay on the cobblestone street, a few feet apart. The Saxon wasn't moving.

Painfully, Mobutu dragged himself over to his fallen enemy. The Saxon had been much stronger than expected and had fought hard. No matter, it ended here. As he reached his victim he began to gloat. "You fought well, Saxon, but now you die. I will drink your blood and it will sustain me, heal me. After I dispose of your head I shall seek out the fat Russian." He plunged his fangs toward his victim's throat.

The fangs didn't reach their target. A huge hand closed on his neck and a fist crashed into the bridge of his nose shattering it. The fist struck again and again. With a mighty effort he wrenched free of the Saxon's grip and crawled away. Suddenly terrified, he swept the blood from his eyes to see the big man rise to his feet.

"What think you, Mobutu? Will Odin welcome you to His hall, or will he send you straight to Hel?" Whimpering in terror, Mobutu crawled away as fast as he could. He glanced back to see the Saxon take a step towards him. He redoubled his efforts and disappeared around a corner. He didn't see Harald collapse to the ground and lie still.

Someone else had seen him fall though. Two ruffians crept out of hiding and approached the body lying in the street. One followed Mobutu while the other bent over Harald. He took the man's wallet then rolled him over to see if he had any other valuables on him. The leonine face made him gasp and pull back, but the creature did not move. Cautiously he moved closer and began to poke through the man's pockets. "Wonder w'ot the 'ell you are, mate," he muttered as he fished out Harald's watch.

"Something very different from you," rumbled a deep voice as a huge hand seized him by the neck and pulled him close. He tried to scream, but long fangs bit deep and closed off all sound. The robber fought and struggled but there was no escape. As the lifeblood left his body he went limp. Harald shoved the bloodless body aside and rose to his feet. His wounds were already healing. He would need to feed again soon, but for now he could function.

Dragging the body of his victim, Harald set out after Mobutu. He found another drained corpse where Mobutu had fed. Now burdened by two bodies, he followed the scent to the river. It ended there. Cursing in Old Saxon, Harald flung the dead men into the water then went hunting.

Three days later a big man stood silently gazing at the burned out hulk of the home where Ella and John West had lived. The fire had been out for many years; there was no fresh scent anywhere. With slumping shoulders he turned away. Harald would send a message to Moscow to warn Peter.

Meanwhile, Mobutu fled back into Africa to rebuild his courage. For nearly a generation he nursed his hatred of all others like him and vented his rage against the peoples of that faraway land.

Bones

Many years passed quietly in the English countryside, but when land developers came to that lonely place, something began to awaken.

Two men in white hard hats stood at the edge of a construction site, worried looks on their faces. The man in the business suit spoke first. "Bones? You're joking. Tell me you're having me on."

"Sorry, Jim, it's no joke," replied the man in the plaid shirt. "The police are on their way."

"God, I hope it's just a murder."

"Jim?"

"If it is a crime scene we'll be back to work in a few days, Carl. If it turns out to be an ancient burial site, the damned archaeologists will be here for years. The whole project will grind to a halt. We'll be bankrupt and on the dole within weeks. If it's just a murder we can still complete in 1984."

"If I'd known, Jim, I would have just buried the damned bones and..."

"The police are here, Mr. Jackson..."

"Mr. Jackson, I'm Detective Marcos, and this is Officer Leary," declared a thin sallow man in a cheap suit, as he approached the two men. "Now, show me the body, if you would."

"It's not actually a body," replied Carl, as he led the way into the main digging area, "it's just a pile of bones."

"Ok, so if it's not a body, why did you call us?"

"There's no head," Carl, stepped aside to show the rotten pine box and the bones contained therein.

"This looks pretty damned old," grunted Officer Leary. "You want me to call the university?"

"Yeah, I guess you'd better call Hank," replied the detective, "just in case. Now, let's take a look. This all you lads found? No clothing, jewelry or anything."

"Nope, just the old rotten box with the bones. What do you think? Is it a murder?"

"Maybe a hundred years ago. Are you sure this is all you found?" Carl had no time to answer because there was a scream of terror from one of the workers.

"Aaaahhhhh, aaaahhhh, sweet Jesus Christ..."

"What is it?" demanded the detective as they all rushed over to where the scream had come from.

"That!" spat the workman, as he pointed with the toe of his boot. There, in the dirt, was a metal box containing the missing skull.

"Where did you find that?"

"It was near the bones," sighed the man, as the color began to return to his tanned face. "The box looked like a strong box or something..."

"So you thought you would just check it out for yourself," snarled Carl. "Not planning to share the treasure with the rest of your mates, eh?"

"No, no, honest. I just couldn't help myself. For some reason I just had to open it."

"I'll take that," declared Detective Marcos. He began turning the now closed box over in his hands. "1903. Ok, so this isn't a fresh case, that's for sure. We'll just hang around until the smart guys get here."

Nearly an hour later, a van arrived with the university logo painted on the side. A tall thin man with wispy blonde hair climbed out and approached with a gentle smile. "Hello, Eduardo, what have you got for me today? Something very old and extremely interesting, I hope."

"Well, it is interesting enough alright, Hank. Check this out. The lads found what looks like a grave, but the head was missing. That was found in a different location, in this box."

"Let me see the box."

"Please tell me this isn't some ancient Pictish burial ground," muttered Carl as he watched the thin man inspect the tin box that contained the skull.

"I doubt that," smiled Hank. "I'd say we have a very cold case for Eduardo. Did you find any other bones or anything?"

"Nope, just this lot."

"What was here before?"

"They say there was an old mansion here once, but the plot has been empty as long as I can remember. I remember my Granny talking about vampires and such stalking the area."

"Well, I'd say you can keep working lads. Nothing here looks like a heritage site to me. You want me to have a long look at the bones, Eduardo?"

"Thanks, Hank. Check them out and let me know if they're worth wasting taxpayer's money over. God, it wasn't enough they killed thousands as witches; they had to murder this poor soul as a vampire. Thank god for a more enlightened age."

"I couldn't agree more," sighed Hank. "Can you guys give me a hand to get the bones into the back of my van?"

"RIGHT, WE HAVE THE skeleton of a female, tall, about five ten or better I'd say," mused Hank Cameron as he finished laying out the bones on the table in his lab. He had arranged the bones in proper order, but had set aside the skull. "Now just who were you, sweet lady, and why did they cut you up like this? Better yet, why was your pretty head buried separately from the rest of your body? Ah well, a question for another day. Perhaps that's how they thought you killed a vampire." Resisting the unreasonable compulsion to reattach the skull, Hank gave a deep sigh as he pulled on his coat and headed for the door.

"Not working late tonight, Professor Cameron?" asked a bright-eyed young woman as he exited the lab.

"Not tonight, Sheryl. There's a frozen dinner at home with my name on it."

"Shall I tidy up the lab before I go home?"

"That would be great, Sheryl. Don't be too fussy, just give it a quick brush then scoot. It's Friday night, and you're far too young to be working late on a Friday."

"I heard that," she laughed as he disappeared through the door.

Singing to herself, she went into the lab and began to sweep the floor. She emptied the garbage, rearranged the tools in proper order, and then stopped to take a closer look at the skeleton on the table. "Wow, girl, somebody took a serious dislike to you, didn't they?" she mused as she first inspected the bones. Sheryl picked up the skull. For some reason she couldn't name, she was compelled to reattach it to the rest of the skeleton. "I'll just put this back where it belongs."

Gently the girl set the skull at the top of the neck and slid it closer. Suddenly it seemed to move in her hands, and there was a clear clicking sound as it locked to the neck bones. Sheryl gasped and jerked her hands away, slicing her finger open on the teeth as she did so. There was blood all over the oddly sharp teeth of the skull. "Darn it," she muttered, "I'd better get a bandage on this, and then clean the blood off that skull before Professor Cameron sees it."

She hurried out to the small office to search for a bandage. A few moments later she returned to see the skull completely clean. Where the teeth had been smeared with dirt and her blood moments before, they were now white and gleaming. In fact, all the bones seemed to be fresher than before. "This is completely nuts," muttered the girl as she put her hand to her forehead. "I don't feel so good. I think I'll just go home and go to bed."

Awakened

As the bemused young woman walked to her bus stop, something in the lab returned to full awareness once again. There was a clear and demanding need, as well as great pain. Blood was needed, for the hunger was unbearable. The pain went on and on as something searched for living tissue with which to repair itself.

The lab assistant returned the next day, but she didn't enter the work room where the bones lay. Sheryl remained in her small office, working uneasily at the computer. She stayed only for an hour before her unease turned to full blown unreasoning fear, and she felt deathly ill. Once again she abandoned the building.

There was almost a moan of protest as the girl fled, but it had been enough. Sheryl had carried far too much body tissue for years, and now finally got her wish. By the time she arrived home again, she realized her clothes were falling off her. In disbelief she stared at the scales which read sixty pounds lighter than they had three days before.

Back in the lab, flesh was now beginning to clothe the bones once again. A young couple who had stopped to snuggle behind the building, suddenly felt ill and fled. An elderly man who stopped to rest on the front steps, also became ill and left.

All through the weekend passers-by contributed life force, and living cells to sooth the burning need. By Sunday morning she was whole once again. Now the need was for blood, and it was driving her nearly to insanity.

She fought the need and lay still on the lab table, listening with all her power. The language was familiar for the most part, but it was apparent that much time had passed. The use of this language had evolved, as had the rest of the world. She listened and learned while she fought the deep burning need for blood.

Darkness fell, and she rose gracefully from the table where she lay. She would now hunt. "*Wait!*" her mind screamed. The young one who fed her renewal might yet return, and it would be best not to venture out until more was known of this world she had been returned to. Alone in the darkness, she waited, waited and fought the need to hunt, the thirst for blood, the mad desire to kill. She waited and remembered.

Her thoughts ran back to the night of the burning sky and the great cat. Ages of hunting and migrating along the slowly changing ice walls flowed through her mind. Thousands of times she had rejoined the humans, but each time she had been forced to move on. As the humans evolved so had she, constantly mimicking their appearance. She would do the same again.

Humanity discovered agriculture and began to develop permanent communities. She liked this, and enjoyed being among them, but each time her need to hunt would eventually result in her expulsion. At other times, her resistance to disease, or her refusal to age, would make her suspect. As religions developed, she would sometimes be worshiped as a god, or reviled as a demon.

More than once humans had engineered her death, but each time she had renewed and arisen stronger than before; and so she had once again. This time it had taken longer, for she had gotten careless and trusted the wrong people. Damn that Bram Stoker, there would be a reckoning for that betrayal. Alas, Stoker was probably long since dead anyway. Mobutu would join him when she found him again.

All through the long night she fought the burning desire to hunt, combing her memories instead. She remembered everything, reviewed it all, mourned the loss of a few special lovers, and then renewed her vows to her own code. As dawn began to pink the sky, she pulled on the lab coat she found hanging on the peg. Best to greet any guests properly attired.

It was just as she heard someone opening the outer door that she caught a glimpse of her appearance in the window. It was as though she and the great cat had just merged. It would be days before she could alter herself to match the people of this century.

She needed blood from the humans of this age if she was to mimic their appearance. Ah well, it was as it had always been. She would regain the power to adjust her appearance once she had drunk her fill. Suddenly she faded into the shadows. Someone was coming.

Out in the outer office Hank Cameron paused, his dormant survival instincts screaming at him to run. Thrusting the urge aside with a snort of derision, he approached his lab and entered. As the door swung shut behind him several things accosted his mind at once, and his mind was painfully slow to process the information.

The bones on the table were missing. A quick glance about revealed a tall woman wearing only his lab coat, standing before the closed door. His terrified mind screamed at him to flee, even as it tried to understand that her face was extremely feline, and she had very long fangs like a saber-toothed tiger. His body didn't respond to his mind's cry for flight in time. With a tigerish leap, she was on him.

Hank tried to scream, but her hand closed on his mouth, silencing any sound. He struggled in vain as her fangs bit deeply into his neck. She moaned with delight as his hot blood squirted into her mouth and fed her starving body. She drank deeply for a moment then thrust him away, fighting the desire to drink him dry.

"Aaahhh, ow, ow, ow. God dammit, that truly hurts."

"Oh don't whine," she admonished, as she finally regained control of her primitive drives. "You'll live. See, even now the wound has sealed. There's something in my saliva that heals. It probably won't even scar.

Drink plenty of water and eat red meat for a few days; you'll be as good as new."

"Just what the hell are you?" he asked, holding his hand over the wound on his neck. It had already stopped bleeding.

"Something very different from you," she sighed as she absent-mindedly licked the last few drops of blood from her lips. He watched in amazement as her fangs receded until they were barely noticeable. "I need a few days, and some nourishment, then my appearance will more closely resemble the women of this age. I must thank you for the donation to the greater good. May I ask your name, good sir?"

"I'm Hank Cameron," he replied softly in a puzzled voice, "Professor Hank Cameron."

"I do beg forgiveness for my less than demure behavior, Professor Cameron," she smiled as she offered her hand.

It was at that instant the outer door opened and Sheryl breezed in. "Professor Cameron I..." She stopped in horror as she saw the woman in the room with the professor lying on the floor. She tried to run but wasn't successful.

"*Come to me*," demanded the strange woman, speaking in a deep hollow voice that could not have come from a human throat, a voice that was truly terrifying. Unable to resist, Sheryl came into the room. "*Close the door.*" Trembling, she did as she was commanded. "*What is your name?*"

"Sheryl," she replied as though in a trance.

"*Look at me closely, Sheryl.*" She did so. "*I need appropriate clothing. Go forth and acquire the things I need, and then bring them to me here. Do not speak of me to anyone.*" Without a word Sheryl turned and left the building.

"Once she returns, I will make her forget all that she has seen, Mr. Cameron."

"What happened to her?"

"She will obey me. She cannot refuse the compulsion."

"Her body...?"

"Sheryl donated considerable life force to my revival, Mr. Cameron. She will need a few days to recover fully. However, her body will never recover its former stature, I'm afraid."

"I'm sure she won't mind at all."

"Women of this age prefer to be slim?"

"They do."

"I'm quite grateful for that, for I much prefer to be fit myself. Far too often in the past I have had to disguise my, shall we say, more athletic figure?"

"Are you a vampire?" he blurted out before he could stop himself.

"Yes, I suppose you could say that I am just that, although I despise the label. Damn that Bram Stoker anyway, both he and Mobutu, the traitorous bastards."

"Ma'am?"

"Yes, Mr. Cameron?"

"Are you going to kill me?"

"I do not kill innocents, sir," she sighed in reply as she allowed her body posture to relax. "I beg forgiveness for the attack. Had I been well nourished it would never have happened at all, but I was near death and madness from starvation. I took only what I needed to survive."

"What are you going to do with us?"

"Sheryl will bring clothing to me, then she will forget I was ever here. She'll go about her business and ignore my presence completely. Sheryl will not remember me at all."

"And me?"

"You sir, are another matter. I spared your life when I could have taken it. I now ask for your favor in return. There is much I need to know about the world as it is now. I need a safe haven in which to rest until I've changed my appearance, and until I've learned the things I need to know. Will you help me?"

"Why not just compel me as you did Sheryl?"

"I could do this for certain, but it would be difficult at best. One who is under compulsion will not volunteer information. If I don't know the right questions to ask, then I will not receive the correct knowledge. Do you understand?"

"Yes, but how can you trust me? I might deceive you and..."

"That would be a serious mistake, sir. Keep faith with me, and all will be well. Betray me at your own risk."

"But you wouldn't know until it was too late..."

She gazed into his eyes for a long moment before she spoke again. "Your arguments would seem to leave me no alternative except to kill or compel you, Professor Cameron. Is this what you wish me to do? I think not. You seem like an honorable man sir, is this true?"

"I like to think so..."

"Then I offer you this bargain; help me and I will do all in my power to remain unknown and unseen in your society. I will not kill, and I'll feed only as necessary for my survival. Once we deem me ready for the world as it is now, I will abandon your city forever."

"And if I refuse, or betray you?"

"I'll go on a killing spree the like of which has not been seen in these lands for centuries. Betray me and I'll massacre half this city, beginning with Sheryl, but I'll leave you alive to see it. This is the bargain, and the price of deception. What will you do?"

"I have no choice at all, do I? I must help you, to save the people of this city."

"Indeed you must."

"So what do you want me to do?" he asked softly, tears in his eyes as he accepted the fullness of his surrender.

"First I want you to stop sniveling and get on your feet. I've promised to be on best behavior and so I shall." She offered her hand and helped him to his feet. "There, that's better. Now, first I'll need a name and papers."

"Papers?"

"Identity papers."

"Of course, you need an ID."

"You appear to be an intelligent man, Hank Cameron. I shall allow you to take the lead in this matter. What must I do first?"

"Well, the best way for you to learn a bit about the world as it is now would be from watching the telly."

"What is a telly?"

"There's a small one in the outer office. May I bring it here?"

"You may."

Hank scurried away then swiftly returned with a small television. He set it up then tried to explain while she watched. Enthralled, she was still watching hours later when Sheryl returned with clothing for her. It actually fit rather well.

"*Attend me, Sheryl*," she said in that terrible commanding voice. The girl came to her, and she fought the urge to drink the woman dry. "*You will forget that you have ever seen me, or the bones that once lay on that table. Do you understand?*"

"Forget..."

"*From this moment forward you will neither see me, nor hear my voice unless I command it to be so. If you see Mr. Cameron talking to himself, you will ignore it.*"

"Ignore..."

"*Very good, Sheryl. Now go back to your regular appointed tasks.*" Without a word or a backward glance, the girl turned and went to her desk and set to work. She was smiling and humming to herself as she busied about with the daily mail.

"And now, Mr. Cameron, how shall we proceed?"

"You should remain here until after dark. Once it is dark I can smuggle you out to the auto and take you to my home. I live alone, so you will be safe and unobserved there."

"Very good, sir. I'll remain here, out of the sun, while you go about your daily routine."

"Ma'am?"

"Yes?"

"What name shall I call you?"

The look on her face was far away, and for a moment her eyes almost misted over. "I have worn a thousand names or more, but you may call me Ella West. That's the name I bore when I was murdered this last time. Those who knew me then will surely have perished by now."

"You were murdered?"

"Yes. Oh yes, Mr. Cameron, I can be overcome, but it's truly difficult. I've been murdered three times, executed as a witch twice, and died a few accidental deaths, but always I return stronger than before. This last time I trusted the wrong man. Rest assured, sir that will not happen again."

"So that's why the skull was buried away from the rest of the bones."

"Indeed, and it did work for a time, but as always before, I have returned. Now then, good sir, let us proceed with the day."

Hank Cameron did his best to go through a normal day while she watched the television with fascination, her insatiable mind soaking up information at an incredible rate. Evening came and Sheryl wished him a good night as she took her coat from the rack and danced through the door. She had completely ignored the tall woman standing right beside her.

Once darkness fell, Hank took the woman's arm and escorted her to his car, then drove her to his home. "Do you need anything special for...?"

"I do not sleep in a coffin, sir," she smiled, her fangs gleaming in the light. "A bed will do nicely. I require only simple comforts for now. Just point me to your telly then go about your business as usual."

Hank showed her the guest room before setting her up with the television in the living room. He then retired to the kitchen for a meal.

Hank went to bed to read soon after that, but his mind would not focus on the pages. Eventually he turned off the light for the night. He prayed fervently in the darkness, until finally sleep claimed him, and gave his troubled mind some peace.

As soon as his breathing deepened she went to her room, shed her clothing, and slipped open the window. A moment later a huge beast slipped into the shadows and away from the house. Once again the saber-toothed tiger hunted the land as it had done ages before.

Hank's house was near a small patch of forest, and the beast slipped into the shadows of the trees. As in times past, she circled downwind until she caught a fresh scent. This was a small herd of domestic cattle, but it would do nicely. Flattening herself against the ground, she waited near the stream. Finally her patience was rewarded.

The ragged herd of cattle slowly approached the stream, vague shadows in the moonlight. The steer was the last in line as they reached the water. Suddenly a huge shadow rose silently and pounced. The steer was knocked to the ground and pinned there, thrashing and moaning futilely as sharp fangs bit deeply.

Blood poured into the cat's maw and she drank greedily as the rest of the cattle fled. Finally she pulled away, the steer still alive. She dared not kill it, as that would arouse the hue and cry. Weakly it struggled to its feet, as the great cat slunk into the shadows and vanished into the night. She needed more blood to complete the recovery, human blood so she could mimic their appearance. Silently she padded towards the city.

The big cat had a bit of difficulty avoiding the lights, but she made it into a busier area where she transformed back into the woman. The sight of a naked woman soon attracted the right kind of attention. As the man dragged her into the darkened alley he had no idea his fate would soon be upon him, for she was losing the battle with the killing lust.

He had no time to scream as she turned in his hands and bit deeply. He tried to scream, but her jaws bit down hard on his throat and she gave in to the desire to drink him dry. A few moments later, she stood wondering what to do about the body. Wait, she had scented Africa earlier, there must be a zoo nearly. Perhaps back in that park she had passed. Returning to the form of the tiger, she scooped the body up in her jaws.

Morning came and Hank found her in the living room, watching a news story about a local thug who had been found in the lion's compound at the zoo. The man had been completely torn apart. She smiled up in greeting, and Hank was amazed to see that her face was now almost completely human.

History

For several months Hank served her need for information, and she soaked up every bit of it. Every morning he checked the newspaper, looking for evidence of mysterious killings, but there were none. She had kept her word, and he began to relax with her. It was now almost impossible to see any resemblance to the woman who had attacked him in his lab, and her more normal appearance also helped him to relax.

Ella had gone to work with Hank one day and introduced herself to Sheryl. Hank was terrified for the girl, but it soon became apparent that Ella just wanted a shopping buddy. He had no idea where she was getting the money, nor did he want to know. He was also blissfully unaware of how she was feeding herself, but again, he really didn't want to know.

One day Hank came home early to hear her singing softly to herself. He had no idea what language it was, for she seemed to know several, but he was enchanted with the richness of her voice and the lilting melody. "Hello, Hank, you're home early," she smiled as she spotted him standing in the doorway.

"Yes. Ella, may I ask what language that was? It was a beautiful song, and you have a wonderful voice."

"Why thank you, Professor Cameron. I did study music in Vienna some time ago. I eventually left because that little creep Mozart couldn't keep his hands off me. He was lucky he was so talented. I couldn't bring myself to kill him. In answer to your question, Hank, that language is from the area you call northern Spain now. It has not been spoken for over fifteen thousand years or more." The wistful look on his face brought her a rare moment of compassion. "What is it, Hank?"

"It's you, Miss Ella West," he sighed as he sank into a living room chair. "All my life I've been completely fascinated with ancient cultures, the peoples of the time before civilization, how they lived, and what their lives were like. I mean, we can try to understand what it was like, but we can never truly know for sure. You have firsthand knowledge of so many of these cultures, and I..."

"Would like to pick my brain? Alright, Hank, I'll make you a deal. You teach me to drive an auto, and I'll tell you all I know of any one ancient culture in which I have lived. Is it a deal?"

"Are you serious, Miss West?"

"Quite serious, Mr. Cameron."

"Why do you want to know how to drive?"

"I do believe it will be a useful skill to have in this era. Also, I can't turn myself into a bat, nor can I fly, so I'll need some other form of transportation. Damn that Bram Stoker anyway."

"May I ask what you have against Bram Stoker? I have heard you disparage his name on several occasions."

With a deep sigh she relented. "Long ago, I met and exceptional woman. I shared much with her, but, unbeknownst to me she was twisting it into something vile, and repeating it all to her weak and sickly son, as bedtime stories. His name was Abraham Stoker. I lost track of them for a while, and by the time I realized what he had done, it was too late. The book was widespread, and the fear it generated eventually brought about my murder. Now then, back to the driving lessons, can we start tonight?"

"Yes, of course."

"Very well, sir, we have a few hours to kill before it grows dark enough for my comfort. Make yourself something to eat, and then ask what you will. I'll answer where I can."

She was relaxing in the living room when he returned with a sandwich and a glass of water. "Can I ask about the people who spoke the language of that song?" he asked around a mouthful of peanut butter sandwich.

"They called themselves the Tulana. They were a peaceful folk, hunter-gathers for the most part, but beginning to get a glimmer of the possibilities of agriculture."

"Agriculture? You said they vanished fifteen thousand years ago. That would push back the discovery of agriculture by five thousand years or more."

"Relax, Mr. Cameron," she laughed. "The discovery of growing crops wasn't managed on August tenth, eight thousand and six BCE. It was a very long process with a multitude of ups and downs, and no, the Tulana weren't the first I saw attempting the process, nor were they the last. I quite liked those folk and enjoyed my time with them."

"What were they like, what did they eat, what was their main food source, their shelter, religion? Did they build homes or live in caves? What did they look like, what happened to them?"

"Easy, Hank, easy," she laughed. "I swear you'd drink my memories as greedily as I drank your blood. Alright, they were a very clever and curious people, the Tulana. They ate many forms of vegetation as well as all the meat they could acquire -mostly rabbits and other small game. They ate bird's eggs in season, what fish they could catch, and several forms of insects.

"They preferred to shelter in caves but could make small huts of animal skins and vegetation, if they had the need. They were somewhat migratory, but mostly remained in the general area of northern Spain/southern France. There were several small family groups of them, and for the most part they kept to themselves."

"For the most part?"

"Yes, once each turning of the seasons, right around the longest day, they would all gather at one special place. At this time ideas were exchanged, mates were chosen, tales told and retold, rituals of union performed, and then they would separate for another year."

"They actually sound quite advanced for that time period. What ever happened to them?"

"Most of them were killed in a single night. The few who survived fled the area and never returned. They were scattered to the four winds, what was left of them," she replied, a note of regret in her voice, "and I never found them again."

"Killed? Was it...?"

"No, Hank, it was not I who killed them, at least not directly. I'll explain. Long before I met the Tulana I created another like me, inadvertently. I had been killed by a rock slide and recovery was slow. Just as I managed to dig my way out of the debris, a young female human happened along.

"Near starvation, I attacked her, but she was savage and I was weakened. I took several wounds. Even as I drank her blood, she got some of mine. I was not as able to control my urges then as I am now, and she was near death when I left her."

"But she lived, like you?"

"Yes, it was several days later that I saw her stalking another human, and stopped her. We fought long and hard, but I was the stronger and managed to subdue her. It took much time, but I managed to teach her about what she had become. I was blind to the reality of the situation, because I had been alone for so long. The idea of a companion like me was very appealing.

"For a time all was well, and we were like sisters, but eventually we got on each other's nerves. We are predators after all, and somewhat territorial, as I then discovered. We separated, and I didn't see her for a long time. I joined with the Tulana and spent many long happy seasons with them. I was careful to hunt far away from the clan, where I wouldn't be seen.

"I returned to the great gathering from one such hunt, to find the carnage she had left. It was easy to tell what had happened, for her scent was everywhere. Carefully, I took the bodies into the great cave; the one with all the special paintings, and the magical things of the wise men in it. I laid them all to rest, and then collapsed the cave mouth. It has yet to be discovered, I believe.

"As for the killer, well, since she couldn't control her urges, I tracked her down and slew her. She revived at least a dozen times over the centuries. The last time I tore the head off and threw it away into a river where the waters carried it away. She did not revive.

"By the time I returned to seek my adopted clan, they were long gone, and the seasons had washed away their trail. Since that time, I haven't heard that language spoken."

"Ella, I am sorry..."

"Do not grieve for me, Hank Cameron, for I've lost more friends and lovers than you could count. It's the way of things for me. Now, would you like to see what they looked like?"

"Yes, oh heavens yes! Can you do that?" he asked, trying to hide the excitement in his voice.

"I can." With a smile, she crossed from her chair to the sofa where she sat beside him. "Look deeply into my eyes, Hank. Release your thoughts to me. See through the eyes of my memory..."

Her eyes were green with a lot of gold flecks in them, and for a moment he thought what beautiful eyes they were. After a moment, her eyes seemed to blur, then he saw a group of primitive humans digging in an open patch of ground. They were small and fairly dark of skin, but with broad shoulders and powerful builds. They wore clothing of sewn animal skins, and had painted their faces with red ochre.

Hank could hear the singsong voices as they chattered amongst themselves, and was surprised to see them look up and smile at him, or was it her in another lifetime? They waved in a friendly manner and went back to their work. It was then he noticed they weren't digging up the plants to eat. They were weeding a primitive garden. Obviously the Tulana had not planted the seeds, because of the random pattern of plants, but they were keeping the weeds down.

Slowly the scene shifted, and there was only a glimpse of dead bodies and then the inside of a cave where there were elaborate wall paintings. The scene shifted again to the outside of the cave and the rock formation above it. "Remember this place, Hank," a voice whispered in his mind. "Remember this place."

The scene faded, and then he was back in his living room with a vampire sitting beside him. His eyes misted over as he thanked her for the experience. "Remember the place, Dr. Cameron, and remember the name. They were the Tulana. The cave remains there undisturbed, or so it was the last time I looked. Before we finally part company, I'll provide you with a map to the area. Once there, you must remember the rock formation above the cave."

"Miss West, you have kept their secret for so very long, why tell me now?"

"You're the first I've found whom I would trust with them, for they were precious to me. I know you'll love them as I once did. They'll be safe with you, Hank Cameron.

"Now then, it's time for my first driving lesson."

Old Money

The driving lessons went well, as did everything she put her hand to. Hank was amazed, but then she'd managed to survive for tens of thousands of years, she had to be intelligent, and resourceful, as well as extremely adaptable. Nearly a year had passed when she returned from a nocturnal hunt to find him waiting for her. Fortunately, she no longer hunted in the sabre-tooth form, so she didn't frighten him to death.

She greeted him as she adjusted her clothing after a rather athletic entrance through an open window. "Good morning, Dr. Cameron, I trust you slept well."

"I heard you leave last night," he said softly, reproachfully.

"Did you have your breakfast this morning, Hank?"

"Yes."

She replied with hard eyes; eyes that were almost feral. "Just as you need to eat, Hank, so must I. The creature that supplied the bacon for your meal waited days in a holding pen, the scent of death all around it, before it was herded to its doom. At least I strike from stealth; the doom is swift and unexpected."

"I know, I know," he sighed as his shoulders slumped.

At that, she relented a bit. "Hank, dear friend, hear me well. I haven't broken faith with you. Out there is a rapist who believes himself to be ill, a disease contracted from one of his victims. He will live on, but his body will remain too frail to harm another ever again."

36

"Why, Ella? Why do you really care? Why not just kill the weakest and eat your fill like any other predator?"

"Because I'm not just any other predator, Hank Cameron," she said as she slowly approached him. "Do not mistake me, sir, it isn't through any fit of compassion or moral code that I do what I do. As I've said before, I'm a predator. In fact, I'm the ultimate predator, and I'm extremely territorial. I will brook no others in my territory, and I have not killed because of our bargain. You've kept faith with me, sir, and I've kept faith with you. Your city has actually become safer because of my presence here."

"I'm sorry, Miss West, please forgive me. I'm..."

"Only human?" she asked with a twinkle in her eye as she gently squeezed his shoulder. She eyed him closely as his shoulders dropped and he sighed deeply. The past year had aged him considerably. It was about time to move on. "Not working today, Hank?"

"No, I'm on annual leave."

"Excuse me?"

"Each year the university insists that I take annual leave, it begins today."

"I see. Do you have any plans?"

"None at all. I didn't know how to broach the subject with you."

"With me?"

"I didn't know if you'd grant permission."

"I see. Had I not been here, what would you have done?"

"I usually take a tour of one or two archaeological sites around the country. This year I had hoped to explore the sites on Orkney."

"You look tired, Hank. Perhaps you should take that trip. Babysitting me has been very hard on you. Go ahead, and I'll remain here to continue my studies. I promise your city will be safe in your absence."

"Are you sure about this?"

"Quite sure, Hank. I will sleep now; when I awaken I expect to be alone. Enjoy yourself and come back to me renewed." With that she turned and disappeared into her room.

Ella lay quietly on the bed and listened. She was acutely aware of every movement he made as he prepared to depart. Only once the sounds of his car disappeared in the distance, did she finally allow herself to sleep. When she awakened she packed a few belongings, and then called Sheryl. All through the night she drove while Sheryl slept in the back seat of her own car.

SHERYL SAT UP AND YAWNED. "Where are we?"

"London. There is a likely hotel nearby, and I will check us in. I have some personal business to attend to, and then I need to catch a few hours sleep. You, my dear friend, have a day to yourself at the shops."

"It would be more fun if you'd come too, Ella."

"Tomorrow, Sheryl, I promise. Today I must attend to some personal business. Here's some cash for your shopping." Sheryl accepted the money without a word, nor did she ask where it came from, or if Ella had eaten anything. She never asked such questions, nor did she ever question the money Ella gave her. Ella checked them in, and then set about her business. Sheryl disappeared into the shopping district.

While Sheryl shopped, Ella sought out familiar landmarks. Fortunately, London is an old city and she was able to find her way. "Well, I'll be," she mused as she found the faded sign on the ancient building. "Thomson and Sons, Barristers and Solicitors since 1763." With a smile playing at her perfect lips, Ella West entered the building.

Inside was a very different story to the façade on the street. It was the epitome of a modern office inside. When asked her business, Ella gave her name and a secret password. After several moments, the receptionist called the senior Mr. Thomson and gave him the name and password. It was a while before he emerged from his office.

"Miss West?"

"I am she. Are you the senior partner here, sir?"

"Yes I am. Jacob Thomson, at your service, Miss West. Please, come into my office." He led her into a plush room and sat her across the desk for himself. "Now then, Miss West. It seems that we must now conclude some business begun by our ancestors. Shall we get the formalities out of the way? I will need to see and confirm your identification."

His mind was unable to register the speed of her movement as she leaped toward him. Her feral golden eyes bored into his, as an inhuman voice springing from her lips. "*Obey me.*"

"Yes," he replied, trembling in fear.

"*When I next speak your name, you will realize that you have already checked my identity, and that you are well satisfied that I am who I say I am.*"

"Yes."

She returned to her chair and sat gracefully, then smiled at him. "Jacob?"

"Yes, Miss West, your identity is in order so we may now proceed. Here is a full accounting of the business as it now stands. As per your ancestor's instructions, we have concentrated a large portion to liquid assets, but we have amassed a rather impressive portfolio as well."

Ella surveyed the report. "Indeed you have, sir. Indeed you have."

"Will you now be taking an active hand in the business, Miss West?"

"You've done amazingly well, sir; I'd be a fool to interfere with you. Please continue as before. I'm actually planning to move abroad, as I have other business interests in America. From time to time, I may contact you with further instructions, but for now I wish you to continue as before."

"Very good, Ma'am. Is there any further business today?"

"Yes, Mr. Thomson, there is. I want you to take a large briefcase to the bank, and withdraw a million pounds in cash for me. Bring the money to me here, and then I will be on my way."

Without a word he placed a call to the bank. A short while later, he arose and left the office. It was over an hour later he returned with a large briefcase which he handed to her.

"Thank you, Mr. Thomson," she smiled as she left his office. "It has been a great pleasure doing business with Thomson and Sons."

Smiling, Ella left the building and hailed a cab. "Take me to a place where I can acquire an illegal identity please," she said as she closed the cab door.

"What???"

"*Obey me*," commanded that terrible voice. "*Do you know of such a place?*"

"Yes," The trembling reply was hesitant.

"You *will take me there, and then forget I was ever in your cab.*"

"Yes Ma'am."

A short while later she was in a small grungy old print shop. She explained what she wanted, and the leering man threatened to call the police. A moment later he had what information he needed and was working. Three hours later she had what she wanted; birth certificates, driver's licenses, and passports, three each, and a passable meal. She paid him his price then left and took a cab to the hotel.

Sheryl slept the night away while Ella prowled the streets. She returned to the hotel near three a.m., her hunger fully satisfied at last. The next day Sheryl packed all her treasures in her car and made the long drive home alone. Three nights later Ella returned in an old car she had purchased. She had made a detour to the West Country to reclaim some more of her property.

TIME HAD PASSED SINCE the murder of Ella West. Humans continued to push forward. We even landed a man on the moon. We became complacent, and vampires receded into myth and legend. The world was far too caught up in its many wars to pay much attention to fairy tales anymore.

Two world wars came and faded into history, several more localized wars as well. With the advances in weapons and technology, a new type of warrior was evolving: Special Forces mercenaries. One such group operating out of Europe was led by a tall blonde woman. One of their assignments was an assassination in Africa in 1984.

On the night in question, the presidential palace was heavily guarded, but the guards were lax. They were paying more attention to the screams coming from within rather than possible incursions from without. Several fell wordlessly to blades wielded by camouflaged soldiers. On silent feet the intruders entered the palace and followed the terrible screams. This dictator had already slaughtered half his own people in horrible ways. He was completely mad, and it was their mission to finish him.

They reached a heavy wooden door. The shrieks came from behind it. The blonde kicked the door in and the team rushed inside. A scene of total horror greeted their eyes. Several women's mangled and maimed bodies hung from chains attached to the walls. In the middle of the room, a victim in his hands and covered in blood, was a demon from hell. The half man half beast turned as they entered.

Shock registered on her face as their eyes met. The maddened creature cackled and licked the blood from its lips. "You! Come to me." With lightning speed it leaped at her, but was instantly cut down by gunfire. Her team emptied several clips into it.

"Mobutu," she breathed softly as she looked at the twitching form, its face returning to a semblance of normal.

"What is that?" asked one of the men.

"Our target," she replied. "Cut off the head and let's go."

Just then a rocket shell hit the palace. Fire broke out and debris was falling everywhere. One man grabbed her arm to drag her away. "Come on, Ariel, the rebels are already here."

"No, we must cut off the head."

Another shell shook the structure. "There's no time, Ariel, no time. He's dead; let's get out of here." Reluctantly she allowed them to drag her away. Ariel was visibly shaken.

Later on the airplane headed back to France, one of the team asked, "Ariel, what was that thing? You've seen something like that before?"

"Yes, I have."

"What is it?"

"Dead," supplied another.

"Oh, it's not dead," she sighed. "It will heal; only cutting off the head will truly kill it."

"What is it?"

"A demon."

"Ha, I don't believe in demons."

"No, then you tell me what it was."

"Africa has all sorts of things I've never seen before. All I care about is that it's dead and we'll get paid."

"Oh, it isn't dead. It'll be looking for us now that it's aware of us. That was our last mission to Africa. We report the mission a failure and I'll pay you from my own resources."

"Ariel, are you certain?"

"Yes, I'm sure, and from this moment on my name is Gudrun. I suggest you change yours as well."

The plane was barely on the ground when she placed her call to England.

"Mobutu?"

"Yes Harald, there was no mistake, it was Mobutu."

"I am Robert now, Ariel."

"Sorry, Robert. I am now Gudrun. Has there been any sign of mother?"

"I caught her scent on the streets of London the other day, but I was unable to find her. She's alive, Gudrun, but where I do not know."

"We must find her before Mobutu finds her."

"Or one of us," sighed Robert. "I'll alert the others and put out some feelers to see if I can locate her."

"She won't be easy to find."

"She never is," he sighed.

"Robert, are you all right? You sound a bit distracted; you need to be focused."

"I'm fine, Gudrun, I just need to feed, that's all."

"Good hunting," she laughed as she broke the connection.

He sighed again, allowing the loneliness seep back into his awareness. It had been over a century since his wife died peacefully in her sleep. The Saxon had mourned for a generation or more, but eventually felt the need for a companion once again.

He had withdrawn to his private sanctuary, gathered the herbs and lit them on the brazier. He bloodied the runes as the shaman of his people had taught him two thousand years or more ago. Once again he called for a mate who could accept him and love him for what he was. A few days later he'd dreamed of a girl child.

HANK RETURNED HOME after two weeks in the Orkneys. The time away from Ella had done him the world of good, and yet tortured him somewhat. He was both terrified of her and fascinated with her as well. Even though there was anticipation at the thought of seeing her, now that he was returning, the fear began to grip his heart once again.

"Hello, Hank, did you enjoy your trip?" she smiled as he entered the house.

"Yes I did, thank you. Were you alright here alone?"

"I've been on my own for thousands of years. Trust me when I say I was fine, however, it is good to see you again." Hank had a strange look on his face, and it prompted her to speak again. "Hank, what is it?"

"Nothing. I'm sorry," he replied as he averted his eyes.

"Never lie to a vampire, Hank." She smiled and gently squeezed his shoulder. "Now tell me, what crossed your mind just then?"

"I just suddenly wondered how old you really are. I mean, you appear to be about thirty, but I know that's impossible."

"Now that leads me perfectly into my next request, Hank. Can you have this carbon dated for me?" She passed him an ivory dagger tied to a thong.

"Of course, but..."

"I took it from the great cat which made me this way, Hank. That is the fang from the same cat that attacked me and made me what I am. I was quite young then, barely grown to a woman. That will tell us both about how old I am."

"This is a sabre-tooth fang," he mused as he turned it over in his hand.

"Yes. A ball of fire fell from the sky that night. I was watching it fall when the long-toothed cat attacked me. The beast was killed by the fireball, and I was drenched by its blood. The next day I awakened fully renewed and thirsting for more blood. It's been the same ever since. Carbon dating that dagger will tell us both much."

"I'll take it with me in the morning," he mused, still turning the object over in his hands. "It shouldn't take more than a few days."

IT WAS A WEEK LATER that Hank came home and returned her saber-toothed dagger. "Well, Hank?"

"I'm still trying to absorb the information myself, Ella." He sighed as he sank into a living room chair.

"Tell me," she urged as she sat near him.

"That tooth is from a species of long toothed cat called Megantereon. It became extinct in Europe nearly a million years ago. According to the carbon dating, that tooth is about one point three million years old. As near as I can tell, your original race was called Homo Heidlbergensis or Homo Ergaster. They were, or so I believe, the ancestors of my own people."

"So, you are saying that I am..."

"Over one point three million years old, my dear Miss West."

She sat very still for several minutes, trying to absorb the information. Without thinking she reached for his arm and squeezed it gently for a moment. "So long ago," she sighed. "So long did I live alone. It's little wonder I was so patient with Terga's madness."

"Terga's madness?"

"The first one I created and eventually had to kill. The change was too much for her mind to handle, and all she wanted to do was kill. It is all too often the way. You see, Hank, there was a time when the loneliness drove me to create others, but I had to kill most of them eventually."

"Most?"

"Some were able to gain control of the killing lust. Once control is established, life has much to offer."

"So there are others?"

"Yes, but as I said before, we're quite territorial, therefore creating another is pointless in the long run, so we rarely bother. It is far easier, and more rewarding, to find companionship among the humans whom we so closely resemble. As far as I know, there is only eight more of my line in existence."

"As far as you know?"

"Forgive me, Hank, but I have been out of circulation for nearly eighty years. There may be more by now."

"You said, of your line?"

"There is also Terga's line as well. In the time we were apart she must have been quite busy. After I killed her I soon discovered another, a male. He too bore the madness and met the same fate at my hands. However, down through time, one or another will suddenly appear, and I must hunt him down."

"Why, Ella? I mean..."

"Why do I care?" she asked as she let her hand fall away from his arm. "I'm the ultimate predator, Hank, make no mistake. A predator doesn't slaughter needlessly. That's the path to extinction for both predator and prey. Call it my way of ensuring the survival of both species."

"Is that all we are to you, Ella, prey?"

She rose swiftly to her feet and began to pace about the room. "Hank, if that was all, then you would have died that day in the lab. I'm offended by that question, especially from a human. How many species has your kind erased from the world in the years that I slept? How many more are close to vanishing forever? You've destroyed the forests, the great open plains, emptied the seas, where am I now to hunt? What species have you left me to hunt, except your own?"

"I'm sorry," he stammered, "I ..."

"Forgive me, Hank." She sighed deeply as she sat beside him once again. "I know it wasn't you personally, however, you do get my point, don't you?"

"Yes I do, Miss West," he sighed as he let his shoulders slump. "If you hunt other species, then humans would hunt you as well. I once thought you to be from the same species as the rest of us, but now I know different. Perhaps your people were the wiser folk after all, and it was only our aggression that allowed us to dominate the planet. That first one you killed, she was one of us, a Homo Sapien, wasn't she?"

"Probably. Ah, Hank, my friend, it's not quite that simple. You see, one people didn't just vanish completely and another appear. The changes came slowly. Only in the past number of centuries has the world begun to change rapidly. Please, forgive my anger, it wasn't meant for you. Now will you please stop calling me 'Miss West' once and for all? I like to think we're friends by now. Please call me Ella."

"Apology accepted, Ella, and now I have one for you. Since we first met I've been completely terrified of you, and you've given me no reason to feel this way."

"Well, I did bite you."

"And, as you predicted, I survived. Ella, I realize from what you just said that I have far more to fear from members of my own species than I do from you. You've kept faith with me, and I do owe you an apology."

"Accepted. Hank, I truly consider us to be friends. In the past year or more you have had ample chance to betray me, but you have kept the faith as well. The time has now come for me to move on and give you back your life. I'd like us to remain in touch though, if that would be acceptable to you."

"I'd like that, Ella, as long as you promise not to bite me again." Hank smiled. "May I ask what you will do now?"

"I swear I'll not bring harm to you. I will now remove myself to North America. I believe I'd like to explore that continent a bit, for I am informed that a distant cousin ruled there for some time." She smiled at his bemusement. "The saber-toothed tiger, Hank, Smilodon."

"Oh, that cousin. Ella, I am sorry, but popular culture paints a very different picture of vampires."

"Yes and the fault is mine. The tales I shared with that woman were tales of those vampires I killed. Little did I know she was twisting, and then relating, the lot to her brat to entertain him. Ah well, I guess I was the author of my own demise."

"This will make your life harder won't it?"

"Oh yes. I'll have to remain hidden, feed so much more carefully, trust none..."

"But you trusted me..." Hank looked directly at Ella.

"I will trust a chosen few, the honorable few, as I've always done. After all, where's the thrill without the risk?" Ella smiled broadly at her friend.

"Actually, you have one great advantage in this new era."

"I do? What might that be?"

"We believe ourselves to be a very world-wise and sophisticated people, Ella. Even if I did tell someone about you, none would believe me. That bit of arrogance will be a great asset to you."

"Thank you for that insight, Hank. I do believe you may be right, but I must be careful to avoid the trap of arrogance myself. Now, I have a gift for you, two in fact."

She rose gracefully and crossed to a small table where a rolled up piece of animal hide lay. Returning to the sofa she passed it to him. "Here's the map I promised. This is a garment I wore when I was with the Tulana. I've drawn the map upon it in the traditional way so it can be more easily authenticated.

"Now, the second gift I have for you is a piece of information I have promised never to reveal. You must not tell that I have shared it with you."

"I promise, Ella," he mused as he continued to gaze at the map in his hand. "What is it?"

"Sheryl is madly in love with you, Hank. No, no, this is not some compulsion I have laid on her; it was there long before I revived."

"Ella..."

"I can see your hesitation, Hank, but trust what I tell you and what she sees in you."

He met her gaze for a moment, and then squared his shoulders. "Ella, can you do me one last favor before you go?"

"Of course, Hank? What is it?"

"Can you give me a compulsion to overcome my self-doubt that a woman like her could be attracted to me? I mean, if you cannot..."

"I do understand, dear friend. Yes, we shall remain friends and stay in touch, and you will love Sheryl.

"*Hear me; you have a deep desire to marry. Sheryl is the woman you desire, Sheryl and Sheryl alone. You will remember what I've done here, but you won't be able to resist the compulsion.*"

"Ella?"

"Yes, dear friend," she smiled in her own voice again.

"Thank you for this. You could have erased all my memories of you."

"You said I was safe to trust, Hank," she replied as she rose to her feet and went to the door, where he saw a pair of travel bags waiting for her, "so I've begun with you. Darkness has fallen, and I'm ready to go now. Come, see me off."

Hank smiled shyly as he approached. "I do believe I'm going to miss you, Ella."

She smiled as she gave him a gentle hug, then took up her bags and walked to her car. "And I shall miss you as well, Hank Cameron."

"Farewell," he called from the doorway. "Don't forget to write."

"I will write," she laughed in reply as she stowed the bags and reached for the car door. "Be well, my friend."

With that she was in the car and gone. Hank sighed deeply in both relief and regret as he closed the door and returned to his living room. "Perhaps I'll call Sheryl," he mused as he reached for the phone.

FOR OVER TWENTY YEARS life was quiet for Ella. For the Saxon it was another matter. Robert first dreamed of a girl about ten years old. Over the centuries he had learned how to direct his dreams and he did all he could to interact with the child. He could be patient while she grew to womanhood.

At first he was always protective of her, and she seemed to be dimly aware of him. When she hit puberty it all went to hell as her psychic abilities began to manifest along with her raging hormones. Robert fought to keep his big brother status in the dreams, but it wasn't easy. He lost a lot of sleep.

As she began using her abilities to help the police in her country, her dreams became violent. Robert always seemed to be there to protect her, but her Viking, as she called him, didn't seem to have any sexual interest at all. That didn't last either.

On her twenty-fifth birthday her aching loneliness caught him by surprise as it invaded his waking hours. Unable to concentrate, he locked his shop early and returned to his bed. That night, as she dreamed, the Viking came to her again. This time he took her in his arms and kissed her deeply. Her body screamed for more as he stripped off her clothes and took her.

The jangling of the special alarm brought Robert alert from that delicious dream. With a half snarl on his lips he checked the message. Emergency conference call. Now!

Robert went to his private desk and punched in the numbers. He put the phone on speaker. "Robert here, is everyone on the line?" Several voices answered in the affirmative. "Very well, Gudrun, you called this meeting; what have you to report?"

"Mobutu's left Africa. My people spotted him boarding a flight to Rome several days ago."

"Why didn't you report this sooner?"

"I was away on a mission; I've just returned."

"Damn, Gina, perhaps you should come to London..."

"Gina isn't on the line, Robert," said a deep voice. "It was my task to contact her, but I was unsuccessful. I believe she's gone mad."

"What?"

"There's been a number of brutal murders in Rome over the past few days."

"That will be Mobutu," sighed Robert. "He's challenging Gina. We have to do something to..." a light was flashing on his phone. "Ah, someone is calling in, it must be Gina." He punched the button to allow the new caller to join the conference.

"Harald Saxon," oozed Mobutu's voice. A woman could be heard whimpering in the background. "I have a little bird here who wants to sing for you."

"Robert, beware..." Gina's voice got no further as a blood chilling scream was torn from her throat as the flesh was ripped from her thigh.

"She sings beautifully, does she not, Saxon?" The screams continued for a while and no one spoke. All except Robert and Gudrun had hung up before the screams finally fell silent. "I've removed the head, Saxon. I'll dump it in the ocean on my way to England. The ancient hag has somehow revived. I will make doubly certain next time. I'll save you for last, Harald Saxon, but you will sing for me too before it is all done..."

He continued to rant, but Robert had already cut the connection. "Gudrun?"

"I have flights already booked for Rome; we board in one hour."

"On my way."

They found the tattered remains of Gina's body in her estate, but the head was not to be found. They swiftly put her in the crypt then returned to London. It was time to track down Ella. Perhaps now Robert could dream about something besides that woman. He needed to focus.

The Team

Sally Connors sat on the riverbank and sighed deeply. She was a woman of about thirty with average looks and figure. In fact, everything about Sally looked average. She would never stand out in a crowd, nor would she ever be considered one of the beautiful people. She made her living running a small New Age shop, teaching meditation and occult classes, giving readings and helping the police find missing people. She was watching now as they dredged the river for the body of a missing child, a child she hoped they would not find, and yet, she knew they would.

Sally shivered, even though it was a warm day. The dream had come again last night. For years Sally had dreamed of a big man with golden hair and long fangs. This man frightened her, for he seemed so real. Sometimes he was a Viking and others he was a shop keeper, but always there were those ageless eyes and that smile. His fangs showed clearly when he smiled in her dreams.

Thankfully the dreams didn't come that often these days, but when they did they were lascivious in the extreme. Recently her Viking was no longer the protective big brother from her childhood dreams. Now he was her lover. Sally shuddered again at the memory of the last night's dream. She could almost feel the touch of his strong hands, gently cupping her breast, his hungry lips searing her mouth.

Lately there had been another new twist; Sally began getting flashes of him during her waking hours. Those glimpses still startled her, yet she longed for more. In the dreams he was often a Viking, but in her waking hours she saw him as a businessman. Could he actually be a real person? She wondered what would happen should they ever meet.

A shout brought her snapping back to the present. "I've got something." It was the voice of the officer in the boat. It proved to be the body of the child in question.

A tall policeman sat down on the bank beside her. "That's another one for your scorecard, Sally."

"I was actually hoping I was wrong, Billy."

"So was I, Sal, so was I. Look that wraps this one up. Can I give you a lift back to the station? We can take care of your fee and get your final statement."

"Sure thing, Billy. That works for me."

"You look tired, Sal," he observed as he installed her in his car then got behind the wheel. She was silent for a long time then sighed and replied to his comment.

"I am tired, Billy, I am."

"You should take a holiday, girl."

"I'm self employed, Billy. That means no vacations, no holidays, no..."

"I get it, I get it," he laughed as he pulled into the parking lot of the police station.

There were two men in dark suits waiting in his office when they arrived.

"I'm Special Agent Mendez, and this is Special Agent Sawchuk; we're with the FBI," announced the older man as the sheriff and Sally entered.

"How very nice for you both," sighed Billy. "Now get your ass out of my chair. So, to what do we owe the pleasure of this visit?"

"May I assume that your companion is the psychic?"

"My name is Sally Connors. I'm in the room; I'm neither deaf nor blind and you may address me directly, Special Agent Mendez."

"As you wish, Ms. Connors," he replied bruskly. "Let me begin by saying that I don't believe in this mumbo jumbo..."

Sally turned her back on the agent. "You have work to do, Billy. I'll just walk back to the shop, and then drop by later for that statement." Without another word she walked out and closed the door behind her.

The sheriff grinned and relaxed back in his chair. "Congratulations, Special Agent Mendez, you have just pissed off the one person who can probably help you. You might as well go home and find another psychic."

"Why do you say that?"

"Sally doesn't like a lot of male posturing bullshit. You got all macho on her and pissed her off. Now she'll ignore your existence completely. You could shoot her in the foot, and she wouldn't even acknowledge you were there."

"Really?"

"Really, now is there anything else I can do for you both?"

"Tell me where to find Ms. Connors," Agent Sawchuk smiled gently.

"She runs a little New Age shop just down the block, Agent Sawchuk. Better take a warrant. She'll just call me to throw you out otherwise."

"He's the one she's angry with. I'll just pour on the charm."

"Try the truth, Agent Sawchuk, she'll know you're trying a snow job."

"Is she really that good, Sheriff?"

"Sally's the best. I didn't believe it either when she first came to me fifteen years ago. She was just a kid, but she was so sure about her vision. She was bang on, so close in fact, we thought she was involved but couldn't prove anything. After she helped us solve about a dozen cases we were all believers. What do you want with Sally anyway, Agent Sawchuk?"

"We're putting together a special team to defeat serial killers, terrorists, and other things of a similar nature. We've got a psychiatrist, a detective, a forensic scientist, a CSI, an electronics magician, a former Navy Seal, a psychologist, and an urban tracker. Every one is the best in the business."

"So you want to add Sally to that team?"

"Our research says she has the highest success average in the country."

"That she has. All right fellas, give it your best shot. Do yourselves a favor though, go easy and keep your opinions to yourself. Sally's a truly gentle soul, but she is Irish, and she won't be bullied."

AS AGENT MENDEZ REACHED for the door to the small shop, Sally dropped the blind from inside and locked the door. She turned the sign from OPEN to CLOSED then went to the counter and called Billy.

Ignoring the pounding on the door, she waited for the sheriff to come on the line. "Hey, Sally, what's up?"

"There are two men trying to break into my shop. I need you to arrest them."

"Sally, you and I both know who..."

"Actually we don't, Billy. I don't know who they are, but they definitely are not FBI."

"You sure, Sal?"

"I'm sure, Billy."

"Be right there." The sheriff sighed as he heaved himself out of his chair. He pulled on his hat, adjusted his belt, and then marched down the street.

"Alright, alright, knock it off," he said as he approached the red faced man who was pounding on Sally's door. "Open up, Sal, it's Billy

Janes." The blind went up, the sign turned to OPEN, and the door unlocked.

"Ms. Connors, we just..."

Agent Mendez got no further as she turned her back and walked away.

"Once again your superlative people skills have won the day, Agent Mendez," said a tall austere looking woman as she approached. "Allow me, if you will." She stepped past the men on the street and into the shop. "Ms. Connors, may I speak with you for a moment please?" She smiled as she approached the counter.

"That depends."

"On what?"

"On whether you plan to lie to me, like those two out there, or not."

"Yes, lying to a psychic would seem to be an exercise in stupidity, wouldn't it? I won't even bother, Ms. Connors. Will you give me a hearing?"

"Sally, my name is Sally."

"Amanda Simmons." She smiled again as she extended her hand.

"Please come in, Amanda. This is where I do readings," smiled Sally as she first shook then released the offered hand. She led the way to a small quiet room containing one table and a few chairs as well as a dozen full bookcases. "It will be private enough. Now, please tell me what's going on?"

"Far too much is going on, Sally." Amanda sat across the table from her hostess as she began. "Those two men actually are agents of the government, but not the FBI. This is a much more secret agency than that, but we do often work closely with the FBI from time to time."

"What do you want with me?"

"Our purpose is to find and stop certain people before they can destroy our society."

"Sorry, I'd make a very poor spy..."

"We aren't spies, Sally. Listen, we're trying to stop serial killers, terrorists, etc. before they can do too much damage. Our team is made up of several professions working together."

"You're a psychiatrist, aren't you?"

"Yes I am. We also have a CSI, a detective, an urban tracker..."

"What's an urban tracker?"

"They used to be called skip tracers. You can run, but you can't hide from Kylie Green. She'll find you no matter where you go. We've got a former Navy Seal and..."

"You want to add a psychic."

"In a nutshell."

"So, which one is Mendez?"

"He is the agent in charge."

"You want me to work for him? Sorry, not a chance in hell, besides, I have a business to run."

"Forgive me for being blunt, Sally, but your business is failing financially, you're close to bankruptcy, and the weight of your gift is wearing you down. Right now you find folks when it is too late. We want you to help us find them while there is still time."

"You people do your research don't you?" Sally was somewhat startled to have a total stranger deliver such a clear assessment of her business and personal situation. She stood up and searched Amanda's face. Her manner may have been matter of fact, but her energy was kind. "Can I sleep on it?"

"Of course, Sally. I shall return in the morning. Sally, we need you, and financially speaking, you need us."

"I won't work for Mendez..."

"I will personally be a buffer between you. If I promise to keep him off your case, will you give it a try?"

"Let me think about it and I'll give you an answer in the morning." Amanda shook her hand and left the shop.

Later that night as Sally climbed into bed she remonstrated herself for being such a coward. "You need the money; take the darn job," she muttered as she flicked off the light.

That night Sally dreamed again of her golden haired Viking. He embraced her passionately, his hands caressing her bare and willing body. Suddenly a demon appeared and attacked them. Her Viking fought the half-man half-beast ferociously, all the while keeping the demon's fangs from her tender body. As hard as the golden haired man fought, the demon was stronger and was wearing him down. As the beasts fangs closed on her lover's throat, Sally awakened screaming and terrified.

"It's just a dream, Sally. He's not real," she muttered as she calmed herself down. "This is foolishness and cowardice. You've got to get over yourself and try living more in the real world. Maybe joining this team and traveling around a bit will shake you out of the rut you're in."

Amanda was waiting for Sally to open the shop. "Just try one case, Sally, please. We will pay three hundred per day plus all your expenses, plus a bonus..."

"Okay, but you promised to keep him off my back. If he starts that macho bullshit again, I'll..."

"I'll stay between you, I swear it. Come on, I'll bring you up to speed while you pack."

"Pack?"

"The job moves around a lot. This case is in New York." Sally had a sudden feeling of deep foreboding, but she pushed it aside.

FAR AWAY IN NEW YORK, a dozen or more police were gathered around yet another victim, a child this time. The body was drained of blood then ripped apart and left where it was sure to be found. Dammit, the media was all over this, they had to come up with something and fast.

In a darkened room, Mobutu gloated as he watched the media coverage of his last kill on television. "I'm in your hunting ground, Old Hag. You know I'm here. Out into the night you must go. Hunt me, even as I hunt you. This time I will not trust a human to get the job done right. I'll dispose of your head myself. Come Hag, I've left my scent for you to follow. Follow that scent to the alleyway; even the cat cannot help you in so tight a space. Come to my trap and die."

THE TALL WOMAN SAT in her quiet, secure loft, brooding over a newspaper. Ella West had been in the city for about twenty years without incident, but now there was a series of suspicious murders. Each victim was found with their throat slashed, but little blood. The Chief of Police was calling the murders the work of a sick individual. "This is obviously the work of someone who is pretending to be a vampire," the Chief was quoted as saying. "We'll find him, don't worry."

Ella sighed as she allowed her paper to slip from her fingers and fall to the floor. She shook her head and ran her fingers through her hair.

"He's not pretending. I know who it is, and I can assure you, Chief, you do not want to find him. Dammit, why did he have to leave Africa anyway? I like it here." She leaned forward and retrieved her paper.

"Alright, Mobutu, you've finally pushed me too far. I put up with you for centuries because you stayed far away from me, but no more. I've returned and was satisfied to leave it alone, but you've invaded my territory, and I won't tolerate that. This time I'll stop you for good; this time you will not return."

Ella sighed deeply then rose to begin pacing about. "I need to think, and I need some air." It was still several hours until dark, but she donned her coat, grabbed her gym bag, and went out anyway. She needed to do something physical to clear her thoughts. Once darkness fell she would hunt, first for nourishment, then for Mobutu.

IT HAD BEEN A LONG flight to New York, but Sally hadn't minded at all. Agents Mendez and Sawchuk had sat by themselves, leaving Sally with Amanda. The two women chatted easily, but Sally knew that Amanda was using every technique her training had given her, to put Sally at ease. Ah well, it was better than listening to Mendez puff up and posture, besides, they were paying her well, and she truly did need the money.

Sally was given only a few moments to rest in the hotel, then she was whisked away to meet the rest of the team. They were gathered in the meeting room of a police station. They were an unusual bunch, but Sally liked them instantly, especially Kylie Green. Kylie had a keen mind, sharp eyes, and a wicked sense of humor.

"Alright people, listen up," barked Mendez as they entered the meeting room. "This is the newest member of the team, Sally Connors. Sally is the psychic you've all heard so much about. Miss Connors, this is Kylie Green, our urban tracker. Tommy Dawson here is our techno geek, Leon Barkley is our Navy Seal, Clyde Markham is the psychologist, and Amanda is our shrink. Oh yeah, this one just arriving is Clara Bynes, our CSI.

"Now people, tea time is over. Report."

The mountain of muscle just grinned and offered his hand to Sally. "Hi Sally, welcome to Bedlam."

"Thank you, Leon."

"I said, report. Green?"

"I got nothing," sighed the tall brunette, "less than nothing. I don't know who this character is, but he leaves no tracks I can find."

"Clara?"

"Okay, the situation is this." The small hawk-like woman said as she adjusted her glasses. "We have a serial killer on the loose. He's fairly new to the city, he's been very busy, he's messy, but in spite of all that, I have nothing we can use. Whoever he is, he makes a mess, I've got plenty of evidence that makes little or no sense, and neither his prints nor his DNA, which is weird in and of itself, is in any database I can access."

"Why do you think he's new in town?" asked Sally.

Leon rose to his feet from his seat on the edge of a desk as he answered her question. "His victims are like nothing we've seen before. The victims have their throats ripped out, and it's obvious they have been tortured, but there is very little blood to be found. The guy thinks he's a vampire or something. He kills for pleasure and then bleeds the victims out. We think he's new because the first victim appeared three months ago. There've been seven in all."

"Eight," declared Agent Sawchuk as he closed his phone. "We've got another one. The locals are holding the crime scene for us. Mount up people."

They all filed out and into a large van that was equipped with a full field lab, plus other equipment. "Okay," sighed Agent Sawchuk, "Clyde, what have you got so far?"

"You want the technical or the regular?" The small bespectacled man with the protruding belly grinned.

"Gimme the regular."

"This is one sick puppy; he kills for fun, he enjoys the experience, he's also extremely intelligent, probably hates his mother, is about early to mid twenties, and that's about it for me."

"Amanda?"

"Ditto to Clyde. This man also considers himself a hunter, a predator if you will."

"Sally?"

"What? You expect me to...?"

"No Sally, I don't. I want to know how it is that you work. What do you need from us?" Sally liked him from the start. Amanda had told her that Agent Sawchuk and Kylie had been the original two members of the team and had been working together for a few years. Sally got a good feeling from them both.

"That depends on what you want me to do, Agent Sawchuk. Do you want me to find this person, or do you want me to find his next victim?"

"Can you do either one? Which would be the most likely choice?"

"If I could touch something of his, maybe I could get an idea about him and/or his location. If not that, perhaps I could get an idea of his next victim. I do have to tell you; this is not an exact science. I..."

"We know, Sally. We aren't expecting miracles; we're just trying to cover all possible angles. We aren't ruling out anything at all."

Just then the van stopped, and a moment later Agent Mendez opened the door from the outside. "The body is inside the house," he said as they all filed out. "Clara, you're up first. Leon, you ride shotgun, the rest of us will go for a coffee."

Sally looked all around then spoke softly. "I'll just stay here and hang around. Maybe I can get some feel for his energy."

"Right," muttered Mendez.

Kylie grinned as she stepped between them. "I'll hang with you, Sally. That is, if I won't mess up your mojo."

"Thanks, Kylie, I'd enjoy the company."

While the others went for coffee, and the CSIs went inside, Sally wandered around the building, staying outside the yellow police tape. They were in an older part of the city, an area that was somewhat run down. Eventually she stopped in the shadows, looking around fearfully. "What is it, Sally?"

"He stood here, Kylie, the killer. He stood here many times, savoring the anticipation. This is truly weird. I know they say he's young, and they're right, but his energy is old, very old. He does hate his mother, and he's terrified of someone else, but he's been driven to challenge that person, or that's the impression I get. The obviousness of his victims is the method of the challenge."

"Cool, anything else?"

"Just his energy, something very old, sick, twisted, extremely deadly, and completely unstable. This one has been killing for a long time. I don't like it here, Kylie..."

"Come on, girl, maybe you can use a coffee at that."

"Yeah, you could be right. Africa."

"Africa?"

"He's from Africa, or has spent a lot of time there."

"I brought you both a coffee," smiled Amanda as they returned to the truck.

"Thanks."

"Any luck?"

"Just some impressions," replied Sally. "Most don't make any sense, but then, that's about par. I believe he stalked his victim for several days before he struck. I also believe he's from Africa."

"Africa?"

"Just an impression, but it was pretty strong. You were right, Amanda, he does hate his mother, but hasn't seen her in ages."

"Alright," grinned Agent Sawchuk. "Kylie, what can you do with that?"

"Okay... young... from Africa... an exchange student maybe? No, not likely, he's way too clever for that. Probably attached to some embassy or other; you know, counting on the immunity and all. It's a place to start anyway, that's more than we had before. I'll go play with the computer for a while."

Kylie set to work, and Sally sank into a seat nearby to nurse her coffee. There was something about the energy of this killer that frightened her more than she would admit. Every instinct she had was screaming at her to run away, but she fought it.

While Sally nursed her coffee and her fears, Kylie worked diligently. Agent Sawchuk watched his friend as she worked, fingers dancing across the keyboard then tapping impatiently when the internet couldn't keep up with her racing thoughts. A slight frown creased her brow as her eyes scanned the information on the screen.

How many times had he seen her like this over the years they had worked together? Kylie was the best hunter in the business, and as an FBI agent he had called her in to consult many times.

When he'd been offered the chance to set up this team, Kylie had been the first person he'd contacted. She'd nearly quit the day the powers that be had given the team to that moron Mendez. He chuckled as he recalled holding her back, trying to talk sense to her. Finally they had gone to a bar to girl watch for an evening, and with a few drinks to calm her down he'd been able to talk her into staying. They'd gone girl watching together many times over the past two years since that day.

"Finding anything, Kylie?" It had been a while and Agent Sawchuk was curious.

"Not yet. Maybe I should find a tall icy-eyed blonde to occupy your mind while I work."

"Now you're talking, sister."

"Go relax, lover boy, I'll let you know when I find something."

Close Encounter

While Kylie worked and bantered gently with Agent Sawchuk, Sally sank into a seat. She finished her coffee, and with nothing better to do, began to meditate. It was a long while later that she suddenly gasped and opened her eyes. She seemed terrified.

Amanda rushed to Sally's side. "What is it, Sally? Did you have a vision?"

"It was a warning." Sally was fighting to regain her breath and to focus.

"A warning?" asked Mendez.

"Yes, a warning. If we continue to pursue this creature there will be more deaths, even from our own number."

"I'll bear that in mind," Mendez snorted.

Sally rose to her feet, bristling at his attitude. "There's more. There is someone in this city far older and more dangerous than the one we're after. She can help us, but she's by far the deadlier of the two. She's hunting the killer also, but I don't know why."

"Any idea who this mysterious person is, or where we can find her?" Agent Sawchuk asked softly.

"None at all, sorry."

"Ah well, this is all so very interesting," sighed Mendez, "but useless. Green, got anything?"

"Too much. I'm trying to narrow it down a bit. Every African nation has delegations coming and going from the UN. I've got a list of the most recent entries into the country, now I'm eliminating all the women as well as the men over forty. This should narrow it down some."

"Keep at it. Maybe the CSIs will learn something new we can use to help you." Sally sank back into the seat but did not try to meditate any further. She was afraid to.

ELLA WALKED SLOWLY away from the sleazy bar. She hadn't actually gone inside, but was just out hunting. Dressed in a slinky outfit with lots of expensive jewelry, and using a very deliberate walk, she would appear to be drunk and easy prey.

The ploy worked, as usual. A man suddenly appeared behind her, put a knife to her throat and dragged her into an alley. "Please don't hurt me," she begged, tugging weakly at his wrist.

"Shaddup and do as you're told, bitch. Make me happy and I just might let you live."

Suddenly her grip tightened so hard that the wrist snapped. She twisted around so fast he had no time to scream before her fangs bit deeply into his neck. He struggled but to no avail. Soon he lay limp in her grasp, and she lowered him to the ground.

"I offer you the same bargain, my friend, and you did please me. *Listen carefully. You will awaken and find yourself alone, injured, and ill. You will not remember how you got here, but you will never return. Your body is ill, and broken. You no longer have the strength to attack another. Remember these instructions. Now sleep.*"

She stood gazing down at his sleeping form for a moment, as she licked the last drop of blood from her lips she spoke aloud. "A reasonable feast, but nothing spectacular. However, I now have more pressing business. There is the matter of Mobutu to deal with."

Ella strode from the alley, all business now. Swiftly she marched the two blocks to her car then sped away. Returning home, she changed into a sweat suit then headed out once again. She cruised the streets all night, but to no avail. At length the rising sun, and her need to rest, forced her to abandon the hunt. She would take it up again at sundown.

She found him a week later, but it was too late, humans had found him first.

IT HAD TAKEN KYLIE a few days, but she'd located her man. First she narrowed down the search to a few young men who had arrived just prior to the first victim. She then eliminated all who had left again. With this smaller list she began to make a few subtle inquiries from the street folk who hung out near the embassies. It did not take long to discover which one had a resident who seemed to enjoy the city's night life, a man who shunned the light of day.

Once Kylie located their quarry, the Team set up surveillance, and again they got lucky. The third night they managed to follow him to a more secluded area. While he stood in the shadows watching his intended prey, he in turn was being watched by the Team. The following night he attacked the victim.

An elderly woman carried her garbage to the curb, when suddenly something charged from the shadows and grabbed her. She tried to scream, but it held her mouth closed as it began to tear at her flesh slowly. She fainted from the pain, just as a huge man hurled himself onto her attacker.

Leon charged from the van and tackled the killer, then got the shock of his life. The man swung him easily into the air and sharp fangs bit deeply as he was tossed around like a rag doll. Leon fought with all his skill, but it did no good at all. Both agents had been right behind him, but he was dead before they joined the fray. Agent Mendez died instantly from the blow to his skull, and Agent Sawchuk felt the terrifying grip and the deep bite of deadly fangs as the half-cat/half-man seized him.

Horrified, the rest of the team looked on as the battle raged. There had been no time to call for back-up. Suddenly, Sally screamed and froze in place as something huge charged from the shadows and entered the fray.

With a sudden terrifying roar, the great cat sprang at the combatants. It was about the size of a lion, but at least twice the thickness, and it was all muscle. The killer instantly dropped Agent Sawchuk and fled from this nightmare out of the ancient past.

The great cat gave chase, but the killer eluded her. She had avoided running down the human woman who was also charging into the battle. He wanted this fight, but on his own terms. She'd nearly got him this time, and she was even more terrifying than he remembered.

Kylie was kneeling beside Agent Sawchuk, trying to stanch the flow of blood from his arm. She looked up to see the beast return. There was no time to flee as it was horrifyingly fast. Suddenly she was nose to nose with a saber-toothed tiger, its fetid breath enveloping her; its feral amber eyes glowing in frustrated anger. It snarled once and then suddenly began to shimmer. Stunned, they all watched as the great cat turned into a tall, naked woman. She was not at all happy.

"What the bloody hell did you people think you were doing?" she demanded as she glared into Kylie's eyes.

Kylie gulped and drew a deep breath before she tried to reply. She did not trust her voice. "We were trying to capture a killer."

"As was I. Give me your coat."

"What???"

"Give me your coat. Do you expect me to stand here naked while the paramedics arrive?"

"What? Oh, sorry; here, put this on." Kylie helped the woman on with the coat as Amanda slowly approached.

"Have you medical training?" Ella demanded as Amanda arrived.

"Yes."

"Tend him. When the ambulance and police arrive, make no reference to me."

"Count on it. I'd be locked up if I told what I saw."

Ella sighed as she turned back to Kylie. "Alright you, take me to your friends."

Kylie led her back towards the lookout, but Ella made a short detour to retrieve her clothes from the car, then they went to the van. "Who is in charge here?" Ella demanded as she dressed herself in a loose fitting sweat suit. The police and ambulance had arrived by this time.

"He's dead," answered Sally, as Ella's eyes fell on her. "It's you isn't it? The one the killer is afraid of?"

"Yes. Now you would be the one whose mind has sought my own several times of late. It was you who found him?"

"No, Kylie found him. I just gave her a clue."

"Who is Kylie?"

"I am." The soft voice came from behind Ella.

Ella turned to take a long hard look at Kylie. The girl was tall, of mostly African heritage, attractive, and although she was obviously frightened, she stood her ground and held Ella's gaze. "Thank you, Kylie, for the loan of your coat," smiled Ella as she returned the garment. "I apologize for my manner when we first met. I confess I'm somewhat less than polite when my prey escapes me."

"No problem." Kylie had been fascinated by this woman from the start, terrified of her, yes, but fascinated none the less. Ella was nearly six feet tall, about thirty, flawless, and of undetermined race. Her hair was long, silky and brown, her eyes green with lots of gold flecks, and the woman's smile was radiant.

Ella smiled as she offered her hand. "I'm Ella West. It seems that we've been stalking the same prey, Kylie. Normally I don't tolerate another predator in my hunting ground, but I believe I'll make an exception in your case."

"Kylie Green," she replied as she tentatively accepted the proffered hand. The woman's grip was firm but gentle, and the coolness of her touch sent a shiver through Kylie. "Can I ask you a question?"

"Later, I promise. Right now the police will want statements. I'd prefer that you folks leave out any reference to my presence here tonight."

"I agree," sighed a small man. "I'm Clyde Markham, and I must agree with you, Miss West. Come people, we'll give statements, make sure they all jive, and we'll keep our mouths shut about our savior here." He led them out to the police where they remained for some time, and then they returned, Agent Sawchuk with them, his arm in a sling.

Kylie was the first to speak as they re-entered the van. "Well, that's done for now. Miss West, this is Agent Sawchuk. He's in charge now. Agent, this is Miss Ella West. She is..."

"The one who saved my ass. Thank you, Miss West. May I ask just what the hell you are, or was I hallucinating when I saw that tiger turn into a naked woman?"

"What I am is of no importance here, people. Tell me now, just what do you know of the creature you're hunting?"

"How about I ask the questions here, lady?" Agent Sawchuk rubbed at the bandages on his neck. "I..."

"*Be silent. Who controls the electronics here?*"

"I do," Tommy stammered softly.

"*Erase all record of me and our interactions.*"

"Yes Ma'am."

"*The rest of you be silent until I speak to you.*" They all fell silent and stood quietly, fearfully, waiting.

"Kylie, talk to me, girl."

At the sound of that rich musical voice, Kylie shook off the trance. "Wow, that's a trick worth learning," she mused softly.

"It has been quite useful in the past, Kylie. Relax, I won't harm you or your friends. I just need information."

"Okay, I'll tell you what I know, then you share with me. Fair?"

"Alright, I'll play fair, but this prey is far too dangerous for you. Leave him to me. Now, who are you people, and what are you doing here?"

"We're a special team, working for a secret government agency. Our task is to locate and capture serial killers, terrorists, etc. Everybody has a special job on the team. Sally is the psychic, Amanda is the shrink, Clyde the profiler, Tommy is the electro-wizard..."

"I get it, so what is your special talent?"

"Hang out with me for a while and find out." It was past her lips before she could catch it.

Ella replied with a delighted smile. "A tempting offer for certain, but there's a more pressing matter to deal with. Perhaps one day in the future. Now, tell me, what is your task on this team?"

"I'm the urban tracker. Give me a name, face, something, and I'll find it. That's what I do, and I'm damned good at what I do."

"I believe you, Kylie. So, it was you who located Mobutu?"

"Yes. What is he anyway?"

"Very dangerous, Kylie. Too dangerous for your people to handle. Forgive me now Kylie, but I must do this. *Obey me, all of you! Hear me well, you do not know of my existence, you no longer want to find this killer, you have other more pressing cases to pursue. I'll leave now, and you will not remember I was here. Tommy, you will remove all trace of my visit. Kylie, write down the place where I can find Mobutu. Once I leave this truck you will all count slowly to one hundred then go about your business.*"

Ella slipped out of the van then stopped to listen. She could hear them counting in unison. She smiled and strode to her car, then drove home for a good day's sleep. She would hunt Mobutu once darkness fell again.

Mobutu himself cowered in his lair beneath the embassy. A shiver of fear ran up his spine again as he realized how close she had come to catching him. How had she managed that? He was laying a new scent for her to follow into a trap, but she been there, how?

And what were these humans doing there? Was she actually working with humans now? No, more likely she had compelled them to help her. No matter, he'd made short work of two of them. "Very well then, Old Hag, I shall acquire a few human allies of my own. I'm not beaten yet, not by half. This will take planning."

He shuddered again as he looked at the freshly healed mark on his leg. She'd nearly had him.

Dreams

For the next two weeks Ella stalked the area, but Mobutu didn't return to the embassy, nor did he make an obvious kill again; he needed time to heal and recover his courage. She'd nearly had him in her claws. He'd shivered at the thought. It had always been his plan to lure her close then attack from hiding. He needed to kill her before she could transform. She was better at this game than he had suspected, and time had not dulled her instincts. He'd gone into hiding.

Ella was growing weary of this game. She knew he was aware of her now, and that he would be twice as dangerous as before. He had gone to ground somewhere else, for his scent was growing fainter at this location. She needed another strategy.

It was a pity about the tall girl, the tracker. Ella could use her skills about now. Ah well, patience would expose her enemy once again. Ever alert, Ella returned to her daily routine.

IN AMERICA, ELLA FUMED in frustration. In London, Robert called his people together. Once the idea of banding together for mutual benefit and protection had been planted in his head, Robert had spared no effort to make it happen.

It hadn't been easy. Vampires are solitary hunters by nature, but the need for survival made them all see the sense in the plan. Robert was a natural leader and the others deferred to him easily enough. He had been a king, after all. If anyone of them was fit to lead now that Ella was gone, it was Robert. The conference call was in progress once more.

"Is everyone in London now?"

"All are here, Robert," Gudrun's voice replied over the phone speaker. "We're all in the same hotel, although we are in separate rooms on different floors. We can all hear you."

"Excellent," he chuckled. "People, we have a situation here. The world is a different place than it was when we were younger. We must change with the times if we're to survive. In the beginning, Ella taught us each to control the burning need to feed, to kill, the mad thirst for blood. Now we must learn to control our natural aversion to the company of our own kind.

"The enemy is at the gate. Mobutu is mad as a hatter and he's strong. He's determined to make an end of us all. We must band together now and work together for our mutual survival. Are we agreed on this?"

"Agreed," replied several voices at once.

"What should we do, Robert?" asked a woman's voice.

"For now, stay here in London. You must hunt in pairs or threes and hunt only as needed. Mobutu is powerful, but he's a coward. He won't attack a group. We need Ella, she's the strongest of us all, she's the most familiar with Mobutu's ways, and their feud goes back long before any of us drew breath."

"It's been so long, Robert; are you certain she's alive?" asked another.

"She's alive and was in London some years ago, but I've been unable to find her here in England."

"We must find her, Robert. Perhaps she can be persuaded to help us and to lead us once again."

"Agreed. All of you stay in the hotel; only hunt in groups. I'll attempt to track her down."

"Forgive me, Robert, but I'm much better at this sort of thing than you are, and you shouldn't risk being caught out alone. Let me accompany you."

"Thank you, Gudrun. I will gladly accept your help. I'll even try to remain civil."

"Such a gentleman," she chuckled.

TWO WEEKS PASSED FOR the Team. The deaths of their two team members had been dealt with, both men's funerals attended, and the team was back in New York.

Agent Sawchuk called the group together in the van/lab once again. "Okay folks, here's the story," he began as he addressed the assembled team. "I've been put in charge of the team. We have a new mandate now. We will no longer attempt to apprehend, we locate only. From now on we're to use local law enforcement to make the final bust. We're just supposed to locate the quarry and gather the evidence for them."

"Hey, that works for me," sighed Clyde. "I have to admit, losing Leon and Agent Mendez that way really shook me up. So, tell me we aren't going back after that thing again."

"No, I managed to talk them out of it. We have other cases to pursue. We also have other matters to deal with right now."

"We do?"

"First, Tommy quit, and we don't have a replacement ready. Kylie, Can you handle that end for a while?"

"I'll do what I can, Boss, but no promises."

"Fair enough. Amanda, you're the best at interpersonal relationships, see what you can do to coax Tommy back for us. Now, Sally, we do need you desperately, but I have to know, are you in or out?"

"I'll stay just as long as we're only trying to find them, and we're letting the guys with guns do the nasty."

"Deal. Okay, here's our next case. The feds believe there's a terrorist cell working in the area, but they don't know who they are, what they're up to, and they don't know where to find them. All they have to go on is a few tips about somebody planning something big."

"Great, so what are we supposed to do with that?" sighed Amanda.

"Who knows? Let's play it like the last time. We'll cruise the city and see if Sally can get a hunch or something. If she can, maybe we can get something going."

"How about Sally and I take my car and go play for a while," suggested Kylie. "It'll be a lot better than staying cooped up in this darned mobile lab."

"Sure, why not. You guys go play while Amanda, Clara, and Clyde go over the current intel. I'll hit the streets. Maybe see what the locals are looking at."

As Kylie led Sally to the car she sighed in relief. They'd come to their senses and put Agent Sawchuk back in charge. She knew he'd be able to hold the team together and he'd also work harder at keeping them alive.

SALLY AND KYLIE CRUISED the city for a couple of days, but to no avail. They were at it again when Sally suddenly broke the silence. "Kylie, what's bothering you, honey?"

"Bothering me? Nothing's bothering me, girl. What makes you think something is bothering me?"

"I'm psychic."

"Right, okay, well, it's really nothing. It's just that I've been having these weird dreams the past few nights. They don't make a lot of sense, but they scare the hell out of me. They seem so real, and they're getting stronger."

"Can you tell me about them?"

"So, you the new shrink on the team?"

"No, I'm just a friend who's concerned."

"Sorry, Sal, didn't mean to get all defensive on you. Well, Leon and Agent Mendez are always in them. Sometimes they get killed by a vampire, sometimes they get killed by a monster, and the last few nights a saber-toothed tiger chased the monster away then turned on me."

"It sounds to me like you are still processing the deaths. Maybe you should talk to Amanda or Clyde..."

"No way, forget that, girl."

"Okay, so tell me the rest of it."

"What??? Okay, okay, I know, you're psychic. Well, there's this woman in the dreams. Sometimes she scares the hell out of me and others she turns me on big time, you know?"

"An old girlfriend maybe?"

Nope. I can tell you; I'd remember this one, and if I'd ever had her I'd never let her go."

"So how does she fit into the dreams?"

"I don't really know. It's like she's really pissed with me, but flirting anyway, and I know that somehow she is keeping the monster, and the tiger, away from me. It's all too weird, Sal honey. Sal, what is it?"

"I don't know, Kylie. Just for a moment I sensed something, something very old, very dangerous, and yet somehow, familiar. Ah well, it's gone now. Look, I'm nearly starved. Can we go back to the hotel now? I doubt we'll get anything this way. Let's grab a bite then check in with the others. Maybe they'll have something that will give me a kick start."

"Works for me, girl. Let's go. Sally, please, not a word about this to the others."

"Lips are sealed as long as you feed me."

"Oh yeah, salad bar, here we come."

THE MEAL AND CONFERENCE did nothing to help, and eventually they retired to bed. Later that night Sally awakened with a scream, she had felt Kylie's nightmare. She rushed to find Kylie awake, and oddly at peace. After many reassurances, Sally returned to her own room and bed. Maybe she could shake her sense of foreboding and find a dream of her Viking lover. An orgasm was exactly what she needed to calm her nerves.

As Kylie slept, she'd dreamed again. This time it was as real as it could get. She felt the terror at the tiger's deafening roar, froze in fear at its horrifying charge, she smelled its hot breath as they went nose to nose, and she watched as the saber-tooth turned into a woman. This time Kylie awakened with a start as her hand touched the woman's hand. None of this had been a dream, it was a memory.

Kylie answered the door and reassured Sally that all was well. She sent her back to her own room, then went to the bathroom and washed her face. Kylie returned to the bed, but opened the curtains first so she could look out at the city. Allowing the memory to wash over her, Kylie sat watching the city that never sleeps, until well into the night. Somewhere out there a vampire was hunting, and now she knew who it was.

The next day Kylie asked for a few days off to look up an old friend. She started where Sally had felt the old dangerous energy. It took her less than a morning to locate the residence of Ella West, an artist who had emigrated from England about twenty years earlier. The woman should be in her fifties, but Kylie knew she would barely pass for thirty. Kylie sat in her car, watching the old building for much of the day, and reviewing the things she'd learned about one Miss Ella West.

ELLA AWAKENED EARLY, keenly aware that something was amiss. Sensing nothing unusual in her immediate surroundings, she arose from her bed. A few moments later she was washed, dressed, and ready for another day. Ella sat to her computer and scanned the area around her building. It took only a moment to spot Kylie.

"Well now, my dark eyed beauty, what are you doing here? Watching for me? Why? Could it be you've remembered our first encounter? It's been centuries since anyone's been able to resist the compulsion. You do intrigue me, Kylie Green. I believe I'll see what you're up to."

Ella rose and swept up her gym bag from the table by the door. Grinning with delight, she took the elevator to the ground floor then marched off down the street, making sure Kylie could easily keep her in sight. She breezed through the gym door, greeted everyone with a cheerful smile, and then headed for the martial arts room at the back. A quick glance over her shoulder showed Kylie Green approaching the information counter.

Kylie followed her quarry into a local gym. She went to the counter while Ella disappeared into the bowels of the fitness center. "Hi there, can I help you tonight?" asked a cheerful young woman, as Kylie reached the counter.

"Sure. Actually, I'm a private detective, and I'm looking for information about that woman who just came in ahead of me."

The girl was instantly wary. "Miss West? What do you want to know?"

Kylie poured on the charm, trying to put the girl at ease. "Anything at all you can tell me."

"I can tell you she owns the place, she's a famous artist or something like that, she's deadly at the martial arts, and she's an extremely private person. I suggest you leave right now, before I call some very large people to escort you out."

Kylie produced a few hundred dollar bills from her pocket. "Look, I know you can't make a lot of money at a job like this..."

"You've got to be joking," sneered the girl. She picked up a microphone and barked a command. "Alex, Carl, Monk, code red, front desk."

"Okay, okay, I'm gone," protested Kylie, as three mountains of muscle came on the run. She beat a fast retreat out the door and took up her observation post again.

An hour later, Ella returned to the street and headed for home, a small grin of delight playing on her face. She stopped off at a convenience store, bought a paper and a lotto ticket, and then continued her way home.

As she disappeared into the building once again, Kylie entered the small store. "Hi there," she smiled as she approached the counter.

"Hi yourself," replied the young fellow behind the counter.

"Can I ask you a few questions?"

"Talk's cheap; fire away."

"That woman who was just in here, do you know her?"

"Miss West? Sort of I guess, why?"

"She come in often?"

"Yep, two or three times a week for as long as I can remember."

"What do you know about her?"

"Not a lot really. She's an artist or something, rich, gorgeous, friendly, and killer on robbers."

"Oh?"

"Yeah. She moved into the neighborhood years ago, and there hasn't been more than two or three robberies in all that time since."

"Why is that, do you think?"

"She's some sort of martial arts Ninja, or something. I saw her take a mugger apart a few years ago. I wouldn't mess with her if I were you. Hey, cool, here she comes now."

Kylie spun around to see Ella walk into the store.

Ella ignored Kylie and went to the cooler where she reached for a container of milk. She brought it to the counter where she called the young man by name as she paid. Turning to leave Ella made full eye contact with Kylie for an instant. She was startled to see the recognition there in the girl's eyes. "Well, I'll be," she mused to herself as she reached the street once again, "she can over-ride the compulsion."

Kylie gave her time to move on before she emerged from the store. She'd been made, no doubt about that. Ella West was toying with her, and had been all night. Suddenly Kylie squared her shoulders and marched right up to Ella's old building. She found a lever and the name West beside it. She gave it a pull and heard a bell ring somewhere inside.

"We need to talk," purred a rich voice right at Kylie's shoulder. She shrieked and tried to leap away, but the wall stopped her progress. Ella was grinning at her as she tried to regain some composure. "I do apologize. I didn't mean to startle you."

"The hell you didn't," gasped Kylie, her hand on her breast. "You did that on purpose, Ella West."

"As you Americans say, busted. Come inside, Kylie, we do need to talk." She opened the old door, then led Kylie into an ancient elevator which rose smoothly without a sound. When it stopped, Ella led Kylie into a beautiful, spacious, modern apartment.

"Nice place," said Kylie admiringly. She was impressed, but terrified at the same time. This was the lair of the beast, and she had no way back out.

"Thank you, Kylie. Please do sit down. Can I get you anything?"

"No thanks, I'm good." Warily Kylie sank into a plush chair.

"You remember, don't you?" Ella sighed as she lowered herself gracefully into a leather chair facing Kylie.

"So it was all real. You did turn into a saber-toothed tiger, and you did make everybody forget."

"Yes, well, everybody except you. What am I going to do with you, Kylie Green?"

"Do with me?" she asked softly, a tremor in her voice that she tried to hide.

"In all my long years, I have known only a handful who could overcome the compulsion."

"How many long years?" Kylie was curious in spite of her fear, and trying desperately to divert the conversation.

"About one point three million, give or take a century or so."

"You're joking..."

"I'm not. I recently asked a friend to carbon date something for me, something I've carried with me since I was quite young. He said it was one point three million years old."

"Wow, and in all that time only a few have been like me?"

"Yes."

"What did you do with them?" Kylie was struggling to keep her voice even.

"Well, in the beginning I just ignored them. I went my way, and they went theirs. They swiftly died of old age or something and were no threat to me at all. They were easy to avoid. In more recent times, I have had to be a bit more creative."

"Creative?"

"Three went on long voyages from which they did not return. Two lived out their days in Bedlam and one I killed outright. You see, Kylie, the times are different now. I can no longer just fade into the forest and go about my business in another area. This is the information age, and I have to be far more careful. You are a special threat."

"Me? How can I be a threat to you?"

"Tell me, Kylie Green, where on this planet could I hide from a hunter of your skill? If you chose to expose me, how could I stop you?"

"Please don't kill me," Kylie begged softly, holding Ella's gaze with her own, "I swear I'll keep your secret."

Ella sighed deeply, almost getting lost in those deep brown liquid pools that gazed so earnestly into her own eyes. The girl was terrified but holding it together. She had courage, as Ella had seen before. "This is very dangerous, Ella," she thought to herself, "but as we said to Hank, where's the thrill without the risk?"

Kylie was terrified, but she held the woman's gaze, begging, pleading with her eyes. Finally Ella spoke again. "Give me an alternative. I truly don't want to harm you, girl. I had so hoped we could meet again and start over, but you remembered, and if I compel you again it will be only a matter of days until the memory returns. Show me another path, one that will keep us safe from each other."

Kylie remained silent for a long moment, gazing into Ella's eyes. The vampire didn't want to hurt her, but felt she had no choice. "Come on, Kylie, think, think, what's the answer? Where is the way out for both of us?" Suddenly it came to her, and as crazy as it was, it was all she could think of.

"We could team up," she suggested tentatively.

"Team up?" Ella was somewhat surprised at that suggestion. She was also impressed at how, faced with the prospect of her own imminent demise, the woman's mind refused to panic. Kylie still had her wits about her, and Ella liked that. "Explain."

"We were both hunting the same monster. I'm willing to bet you still are. I'd also bet that by working together we could find him and bring him down. We'd be great together."

"I'm quite sure we would." Ella was smiling with delight now. "Alright, but what am I supposed to do with you after I've killed Mobutu?"

"Trust me. If we work together on this it'll give us both a chance to prove that we're trustworthy, that we can keep faith with each other."

"Why do I need you to trust me?"

"How many of those million plus years have you spent alone? Having a friend once in a while wouldn't be such a bad thing, would it?"

Ella sighed deeply and melted back into her chair. "So you've deduced my soft spot have you, Kylie? Yes, it does get lonely at times. Girl, I have mourned the death of more lovers and friends than you might be able to imagine. I sense your attraction to me, and I confess you do intrigue me..."

"But you're not sure if you want to go down that road again? How about a friend, someone who knows, but holds the secret sacred? Someone to confide in once in a while?"

Ella didn't respond, she just gazed into those dark eyes for a long moment. Finally she rose and began to pace about the room. Kylie's eyes began to dart about, seeking a possible means of escape, or to overcome her captor. "Don't even think about it, Kylie," sighed Ella as she stood gazing out the window.

"How do you do that?"

"If it were me, I'd be looking for an escape hatch."

Ella returned to her pacing and Kylie wondered if she had blown it. She decided that her only chance of survival was to convince Ella that she could be trusted. "Ella?"

"Yes, Kylie?"

"Are you still willing to consider the idea?"

"That's exactly what I'm doing as we speak." Ella returned to her chair and sat gracefully. "It's the trust thing, girl. It isn't natural for me, and you are facing your possible death, so..."

"You think I'd say or do anything to survive."

"I would."

"Okay, I'll admit it, so would I, but..."

"But?"

"Are you truly considering the idea?"

"Yes."

"But you need a reason to believe you can trust me."

"Precisely, my dear Kylie Green. I could use your skills on this hunt, I'm actually enjoying your company right now, and I do want to find a way to trust you. I believe your idea has merit. Now we must find a way to make it work."

"We need to find enough common ground to form a bond of trust."

"Any suggestions?"

"We could swap life stories."

"That could take a while," laughed Ella. "I believe you may be right though, for the longer we talk, the more I'm trying to find a way to make it work. Alright my young beauty, tell me your story."

Swapping Tales

"Okay, if I must," laughed Kylie, "but compared to you I don't have a lot to tell. I haven't led a very exciting life so far, but I'm in hopes that might change."

"You're stalling, talk or else." Ella's bright smile took the sting from her words and put Kylie more at ease.

"Yes, Ma'am. Well, I was born in New Orleans. My daddy was from France and my mother is from Mississippi. Daddy was there on holiday, and he never went back."

"He enjoyed New Orleans, did he?"

"The short time he was there. He and Mom hit it off and were joined at the hip for days; long enough for her to get pregnant. They were walking home one night when they were attacked by a mugger. In the struggle my father was stabbed. He didn't survive. The mugger was caught but got out on bail and skipped town."

"So you grew up and became a hunter?"

"Yes, indeed. That man robbed me of my father, and all the great things I might have learned from him, the times I could have shared with him. I excelled at school, I studied forensics, and I devoured every detective novel I could find. I got my PI license early and went on the hunt. I got very good at what I do. Eventually I tracked that bastard down and put him away. I've been a hunter ever since."

"No love life? No family? Friends?"

"You've already met my friends. There are a few former lovers; they just couldn't handle the passion I have for my work. I forget everything when I'm on the hunt. The last one was over two years ago. She sure was something, but I left her alone too often I guess."

"So you're lesbian?"

"Yes. Is that a bad thing?"

"Not at all. I'm from a time before time, Kylie, a time before religions or prejudices. Among my own people women and men often found comfort with those of the same gender."

"Did you ever...? I mean..."

"It's time for the condensed version of my story?"

"Oh yeah, tell momma Kylie everything."

Ella smiled in spite of herself. "Very well. I have no idea where I was born, somewhere in Europe I suspect. We were a simple people, living in the great boreal forests, hunting small game, and gleaning whatever we could find for food. We sheltered in caves mostly, or under the branches of the great trees.

"I was large for a child, and I grew faster and stronger than other children. By the time I was of an age to mate, I was too large and too strong. The males feared me, as did the females. One day, in my frustration, I tried too hard and was driven out of the family unit. For many days I tried to survive on my own.

"Alone is, was, not a natural state for my people. I was sitting beside a stream, lamenting my fate, when I noticed a fire in the sky. About that same time, a saber-toothed tiger noticed easy prey, me. The tiger leaped on me just as the meteor struck the ground. I was bathed in blood, both my own as well as the cat's, and radiation of some kind. I fainted, and when I awoke I was as I am now.

"For long ages I followed the great herds, as the ice walls ebbed and flowed. I hunted, slept, and hunted again. From time to time I would join one human group or other, but eventually I always had to move on.

Over time, man evolved and joined in larger and larger social groups. It was easier for me to move among them and thus it was less lonely."

"In the stories, a vampire can make other vamps. Is this true? Could you make a lover with a longer life span?"

"Long ago, Kylie, I discovered that I could do just that. It was an accident, and eventually brought me great pain. The repercussions are still with me, with us all.

"I will explain. I'm a predator. I became this way by accident; another accident caused me to make another predator. This led to several discoveries for me.

"You see, Kylie, when this change comes to a person, there's a driving need for the taste of blood. It is a need and a lust that would make heroin addiction seem unworthy of mention. It's a form of madness, and not everyone can learn to control it, almost none in fact. The first I accidentally created couldn't. Eventually I was forced to kill her.

"Unfortunately, in the time before I did that, she made others. All in her line bear the madness and are somewhat uncontrollable. The one we both hunt is, I believe, I hope, the last of her line. As long as he remained in Africa I ignored him, but he has come here to challenge me, and must be killed."

"You said, 'of her line'. Are there others of your line?"

"There are eight now besides me, I do believe. Most cannot gain control of the killing lust and must be destroyed, but of my line, eight have managed to gain that control and survive."

"Are there any here in...?"

"No Kylie, there are none on this continent, as far as I know. You see, this is one of the things I learned, we are solitary predators, and extremely territorial. If I made you one like me, and even if you gained control, we would soon quarrel, then part in anger, if you survived. At first we would be lovers, but in about a year or so we would quarrel over territory and part.

"That's why there are so few in my line after all this time. It's all so very pointless to make a companion with whom you will spend so little time. It's far better to find a human companion, and spend as much of their lifetime together as possible."

"And then you move on. Ella, you're blessed with so much, but you've paid a heavy price as well. I swear I'll never betray you. Hell, nobody would ever believe me anyway."

"Yes," smiled Ella, "Hank did say human arrogance, and firm belief that they're at the top of the food chain, would serve me well in this time."

"Hank?"

"A dear friend back in England. He's the one who carbon dated my dagger for me. It's a fang I took from the body of the very cat that made me this way. That's his photo right at your elbow."

Curious, Kylie picked up the framed picture and read the inscription. "Best Wishes, Hank, Sheryl, Ella, Tom, and Kimberly. They named their first born after you? So, they know about you?"

"Hank knows. I made Sheryl forget certain things, but Hank is fully aware and has kept my secret well."

"I know this guy. He's that archaeologist who made all those discoveries in Spain when I was a kid. We had to study him in school. Did you...?"

"Well, I did give Hank a few hints. I return to England every year or so to spend a few days with them. I don't do it often, because my presence is hard on Hank."

"He's still afraid of you?"

"At a deep level yes, but he has good reason. You see, Kylie, back in 1907, my husband of the time slipped me a heavy sleeping potion. He then led a group of men into our bed chamber while I lay asleep. They murdered me, dismembered the body, and buried me in secret."

"You're not serious..."

"Quite serious. I have actually died many times, but I always return, and when my bones are freshly clothed in flesh, the need for blood is overpowering. So near was I to blood madness when I revived, I attacked the first human to cross my path."

"Hank, right? But you didn't kill him, Ella."

"No I didn't, and we did become friends, but that first experience stayed with him at a deep level..."

"So you left, rather than trust him completely. He was in love with you, wasn't he?"

"Yes, well, I do have a certain animal magnetism, but no he wasn't."

"Oh yeah, baby. Animal magnetism, I can attest to that," purred Kylie, almost shocked at herself and her own boldness.

"Down, girl, down," laughed Ella. "I'm the predator here, remember?"

"Oops, sorry."

"Don't be, it was delightful, Kylie. Anyway, back to my story. Sheryl worked for Hank and had a wild crush on him..."

"So you made him love her?"

"Not exactly. At his request, I put the compulsion on him to overcome his own self-doubt. Nature looked after the rest. They've been quite happy now for many years. We exchange letters every month. Hank writes one and the next time it's from Sheryl."

"Ella, you realize that you just gave me the means to find you no matter where you go. Does this mean you have decided to kill me, or to trust me?"

"I do not kill innocents, Kylie, nor have I for as long as I can remember; and I can remember a very long time. However, you gave up that designation when you tracked me down."

Kylie looked puzzled and for some reason Ella felt compelled to explain. "I'm a predator, Kylie, an extremely territorial predator. I hunt, yes. I feed as necessary to survive, yes, but I do not prey on innocents. I hunt the other predators in my territory. I feed on the rapists, the muggers, and other forms of violent humans that cross my path, and I rarely ever kill."

"Why?"

"I confess I'm driven to do so, but dead bodies are difficult to explain, whereas unhealthy humans who are confused, are a natural part of the modern landscape. In this way I remain hidden from the general population, and I can enjoy life without always being on the run from angry villagers with sharpened stakes. Those won't actually kill me, by the way, but they do hurt like hell."

"So..."

"Yes, I was trying to find a way that I could avoid having to kill you, my dear. Thank you for the solution to the problem that I couldn't find. I accept your offer to team up, as you put it. So tell me, what's our next step?"

There was no time for Kylie to answer, as several alarms went off at once. Kylie was startled at the speed of Ella's reaction. She was on her feet and at a computer console in a heartbeat, a snarl on her perfect face. Down on the street, right at her door, was the rest of the Team and a full SWAT detail.

"Ella, I didn't..."

"I know, Kylie, it's that blasted psychic. See, there she is with them. Dammit, I really like this place. Somebody is going to pay for me losing it and having to start over. I'll..."

"Wait, let me." Kylie gripped Ella's arm tightly. Suddenly she released her grip as those burning feral eyes turned on her. "You said you wanted to trust me, so trust me now. Let me go down to them. I'll send them away, then come right back to you. You can monitor it all from here. If I mess up, or if I fail, you can still use your escape plan. Please?"

Ella gazed into the girl's eyes for a long moment before she spoke. "Go, I'll be watching."

The elevator door slid silently open and Kylie leaped inside. "Be right back," she sang cheerfully, even though she was trembling all over.

Ella turned on the sound and listened to the conversation on the street. "Sally, are you sure about this?"

"Yes I am. Kylie's in grave danger, but I don't know the nature of the threat. There's an energy in there that's extremely old, and extremely dangerous. The problem is, the danger comes and goes. One moment the threat's real, and the next it's friendly. What I do know, is that we have to get her out of there right now."

"Ma'am, I'm sorry, but we need more than a vague hunch before we can go busting down somebody's door. We need to have probable cause of a crime being committed, or about to be committed. We..."

The big police officer got no further as the old steel door swung open and an angry Kylie burst through. "What the hell are you guys doing here? Have you all gone completely nuts?"

"Sally said you were in danger," stammered Agent Sawchuk, backing away as Kylie advanced on him.

"Do I look like I'm in any danger to you? It's you guys who're in danger. I should shoot the lot of you."

"Kylie, there's something in that building..."

"Yes there is, Sally. The woman of my dreams is in there. I was just starting to get close when every alarm in the country went off. The girl lives alone in a rough neighborhood, for heaven's sake. She has state of the art alarm systems, which you managed to set off and ruin my chances for a perfect evening."

"I think we should be getting back to the station boys," laughed the big policeman. With that the SWAT team left them on their own.

"Kylie..."

"Go home, Sal. Trust me, I'm just fine, it's all right. Go home and leave us in peace."

"Kylie, I can sense..."

"Sally, I know what you sense in there, and I also know it won't hurt me. I'm safe here. Go back to the hotel now and I'll see you in the morning. Right now, I'm going back up to my date, and hope like hell I can repair the evening. Everybody go home and I'll see you in the morning. Okay?"

"Okay, Kylie, I'm sorry we ruined your evening," sighed Agent Sawchuk. "Get lucky."

"Kylie..."

"Go home, Sal," sighed Kylie, as she reached over to give Sally's arm a gentle squeeze. With that she turned and re-entered the building. Amanda led a bewildered Sally back to the car which drove away.

"Ella?" Kylie called softly as the elevator door opened again.

"Right here, Kylie." Ella was still standing at the monitor, making sure the intruders did indeed leave. "Stay here, I'll be right back."

"Where are you going?"

"Roof."

"Ella, they did leave. I know, I know, you need to make sure. Okay, I'll be right here."

Ella disappeared for a few moments then returned to find Kylie back in her chair, waiting patiently. "As you said, they did indeed leave the area. Well done, Kylie. It's not lost on me that you had your chance to escape and didn't take it. Instead you sent them away and protected me. I'm well pleased with you, Kylie Green. You've proven yourself a trustworthy friend."

"Or a gambling fool."

"So, where's the thrill without the risk?"

"I don't know how many more thrills my heart can take in one night."

"Then you must rest. Remain here if you wish and rest."

"Where are you going?"

"I will hunt and feed this night. I must be well nourished, and fully rested if we're to take down Mobutu. I will feed and then rest until tomorrow evening."

"I could come with you."

"No, Kylie," Ella smiled sadly as she lightly brushed the girl's cheek with her fingertips. "This is something I would rather you not see me do, at least not yet. Now it's your turn to trust, Kylie Green."

"Okay, I'll stay here then. I want to be here when you get home."

"The doors will lock behind me. You can reset the alarms at that console over there."

With that Ella stepped into the elevator and vanished from sight. Kylie explored the apartment a bit before settling down in front of the huge TV screen. She waited a long time, but Ella didn't return. Kylie was beginning to wonder if she ever would when sleep claimed her.

The bright sunlight streaming through the window finally awakened Kylie. There was a blanket over her. Rising softly, Kylie found Ella asleep in her bed.

The Team

Ella slept through much of the day then arose to find Kylie still in the apartment. "So, you stayed here all day too?"

"Yes."

"Have you eaten anything yet?"

"I managed to forage a meal from your kitchen. Forgive my ignorance, Ella, but I was under the impression vam..., I mean certain predators, only drank blood. You seem to have a fair amount of food around for..."

"You can say the word, Kylie. I won't bite your head off."

"Well, that is reassuring," giggled Kylie, drawing a rich laugh from Ella.

"I guess vampire is the label I must wear now, and it is my own damned fault."

"Oh? How so?"

"About a century or more ago I became extremely lonely, and trusted too easily. One woman I trusted was the mother of Bram Stoker. She twisted everything I told her, for his entertainment, and he twisted it even further to titillate the general public. I would have much preferred something like cat-woman, or immortal tigress, but I guess vampire it must be. So be it then.

"Now, about the food. Blood nourishes me and sustains me, but I do enjoy a glass of milk and bit of meat from time to time, and occasionally I do have guests, so..."

"Okay, I get it."

"What is it, Kylie? You look disappointed."

"I dunno, I guess I am just a bit disappointed."

"About what?"

"One of my favorite things to do is go out for a nice meal, but it doesn't make a lot of sense to ask you out to dinner, does it?"

"Au contraire, ma cherie. I'd be delighted to join you for dinner. Please don't be offended if I just pick at the food. It's your company I'll enjoy the most."

"Can we do that? I mean, would you really go out with me?"

"Of course. Kylie, Did I misinterpret your intent when you suggested we team up? I had the distinct impression you wanted more than just a professional relationship."

"Well, yes, I mean... O hell, Sally is supposed to be the psychic one around here. Tell me you can't read minds too."

"I can't read minds, girl, but I do have rather keen instincts."

"Ella, why did you agree to do this? Was it just to keep from hurting me? If it was, I will swear any oath you want that..."

"Stop this now, Kylie," soothed Ella as she took Kylie into her arms. "You must know that, had I not been intrigued by you, my decision would have been easy enough for me. The truth is, I was quite desperate to find a path to keeping you alive so we could get better acquainted."

"You're serious?" Kylie had a smile of delight on her face. "You were really interested in me? Why?"

"Fishing for compliments?"

"Shamelessly, so give already."

"It was our first meeting, Kylie. There you were, trying to defend your comrades, facing a nightmare from the distant past, and yet you held your ground. The madness increased as the great beast turned into an angry woman, and still you didn't falter. You have great courage, Kylie, and that did intrigue me.

"After I put the compulsion on your team, I did a bit of checking up on you. I liked what I learned about your courage, your standards of conduct, and especially your skills. I was musing over the fact that I could truly use your help, and was trying to think of a way to introduce myself, when I noticed I was being watched. Imagine both my delight and dismay to find you tracking me."

"Delight and dismay?"

"Delight that you were about to make the introduction very easy for me, and dismay that I might have to hurt you to protect myself. I confess I was pleased that you could see a way out for both of us, Kylie. This will take a bit of adjustment for us, but I think we will do well together."

"I hope so, Ella. So, what do we do now?"

"I think we should spend the evening getting better acquainted."

"Oooh, that works for me."

"You're shameless," laughed Ella. "Decorum, Miss Green, decorum. Give it a bit of time, girl, let it evolve."

"Alright, if I have to. So, as I said before, what now?"

"Well, you could go over my security system and see if you can beef it up a bit. You know something to help me throw off an urban tracker?"

"Right. Okay, let's see what you've got here." Ella pulled aside a panel in the wall and displayed a series of monitors and alarm systems. "Wow, not bad, girl. You got this place tight as Fort Knox. Okay, you're good here, but..."

"Not out there; how did you find me, Kylie?"

"It was way too easy, Ella. First, Sally picked up your energy a few days ago, so I had an area to go with. I asked around a bit and soon had a name. A quick call to Motor Vehicles gave me an address, so I rolled on over and waited to see if I had the right girl. Bingo, a few hours wait and I see the woman of my dreams walk out that door."

"So I was that easy to find. Tell me what I should have done."

"Well, it really didn't matter, or it wouldn't have, if the compulsion thing had worked. Aside from that, you need to make it a bit harder. First, give a false address on all documents, an abandoned building or something like that. Second, have at least two or more spare IDs and change them up often. Third, have an urban tracker on your team to make sure nobody's on your trail."

"Good recommendations all. Do you know where I can find a good tracker looking for a position?"

"Come a little closer, I'll bet you'll see one," purred Kylie.

Ella pulled her close and hugged her gently. "Patience, my darling girl, patience. Let us grow together first."

"Sorry, I don't mean to be pushy."

"I don't find you pushy, Kylie, but I do sense your fear as well as your attraction. I promise we'll become intimate, but first I want to reach the point where you're at ease with me, not afraid of me. You've asked me to trust you, girl, and I have, I do. Now it's your turn to learn to trust."

"I do trust you, Ella, I do..." She shrieked and leaped away as Ella made a sudden movement. "Dammit, West, you did that on purpose," admonished Kylie, as she held her hand to her breast. Ella was chuckling softly. "Okay, I get the point, but..."

"Do not many women marry men who are much larger and stronger? Do these women not trust their safety to the bond between them?"

"Yes they do, and many live to regret it."

"Point taken. Forgive me for frightening you, Kylie, I think we need to take some time to get comfortable with each other. Shall we spend our evenings together, yet return to our normal routines?"

"Okay, I can go slow. Do you trust me to go back to work?"

"Yes. Kylie, is that why you stayed here, to prove trustworthy, to make me feel safe with you?"

"Yes."

"Alright, what must I do to make you feel safe with me?"

"I guess you're right, Ella, I do need time to adjust."

"Stay with me this evening, Kylie. Let's get to know one another better. Return to your home when it grows late, then go to work in the morning as usual."

"I could get a few days more off; I could spend them with you. We could begin the hunt for that thing."

"I want the bond between us to grow stronger first, Kylie. Very well, arrange your time off then come here to me. We'll join ourselves at the hip, as you said of your parents. Perhaps you're the wiser in this."

"It's still early. I'll call Agent Sawchuk and make the arrangements," flashing a grin, "and then go to the hotel and grab some things. Does that work for you, Ella?"

"Yes, Kylie, that would be fine. Go ahead now and do what you must. I'll make room for you in the closet while you're gone."

Kylie made her call then fled to her car.

THE THIN MAN LOOKED surprised and suspicious to see the two tall blonde people at his door. "Yes, can I help you?"

"Please forgive the intrusion, sir, but are you the Hank Cameron who once taught at the local university?"

"I am. How can I help you?"

"I'm Robert Essex. I'm trying to locate a member of my family who's been lost to me for many years. Her name is Ella West, I believe you know her."

"Yes, I know her. Who did you say you were?"

"Obey me!" said the blonde woman as she stepped forward impatiently. *"Give me the address and phone numbers for Ella West. Quickly!"* Hank hastily obeyed. She took the paper and glanced at it. *"You will remember nothing of our visit. There was no one at the door."*

He closed the door and they heard him call out. "There was no one there. I must be hearing things."

As they walked away, Gudrun passed the paper to Robert. "America," he mused.

"Robert, what's wrong?" she asked as they got back in the car.

"Wrong? There's nothing wrong."

"You're a poor liar, Robert. You've been distracted for weeks now, years even. What is going on?"

"Nothing really."

"Robert, we're on the cusp of a combat situation. You're distracted and I need to know that you will not be so should Mobutu suddenly appear. Now tell me what's going on."

"All right, Gudrun, I'll talk, but if you laugh at me, I'll..."

"Just talk to me Robert."

"A number of years ago I started having dreams of a child, a girl. It was always the same girl. As the years passed and she grew, the dreams became stronger until she started invading my waking thoughts as well. She's a grown woman now, and I feel her reach for my mind sometimes. Lately she's been disturbed and frightened. I can feel her unease."

"Really? Ask her if she has a brother, preferably a bit shorter than me with a lot of muscle and an air of gentle authority, a take charge sort of fellow."

"This is no laughing matter; it's real."

"You have a psychic connection with a woman you've never met."

"I believe so."

"All right, Robert, but you need to push it aside until we've dealt with Mobutu, then you can explore it further. Can you do this?"

"Yes I can. I know you're right; I have to focus."

"So, does she have a brother?"

"Piss off, Gudrun."

She smiled wickedly and turned to look out the window. Robert sighed as he drove on. As much as she irritated him, she was one of the finest warriors on the planet and she had been, well before she'd been made vampire over a thousand years ago. There was no other he would rather have at his side in battle, except perhaps Ella West.

IN THE END ELLA AND Kylie spent nearly three full weeks together. The team was getting worried. Sally's premonitions were becoming more frequent by the day as well. Finally she could take no more and persuaded Agent Sawchuk to help her retrieve her friend. Her fears grew stronger as they drove past an old building where Kylie's car had been found, apparently abandoned. They knew this place.

Once again the alarms sounded and Kylie went down to send them away, but this time Sally was having none of it. "No, Kylie, no, you're coming with us. I don't know what the hell is going on here, but there's an energy here that is very old and extremely dangerous. It scares the hell out of me, Kylie. There's a cold blooded killer in that building somewhere, now get in the car. Amanda, help me get her in the car."

"Are you all going crazy?" Kylie pulled her arm from Sally's grasp. "Go away and leave us alone. I promise I'll come back to work tomorrow, now relax, and go home. Okay?"

"It is all right, Kylie," a rich voice purred from the speaker. "Bring your friends up. I'd love to meet them."

Sally gulped as she began backing away. "This is not a good idea..."

"Forget that, Sally." Kylie took Sally by the arm and steered her toward the door. "You owe Ella an apology, and you're going to do it in person." She herded them all into the elevator which rose soundlessly to the top floor.

"Please, do come in, folks," smiled Ella, as she greeted them at the elevator door. She showed them into the living area and sat them all down. "Can I get you something? A drink perhaps? Something to eat?"

"No thanks, we're fine, Miss West," replied a nervous Agent Sawchuk.

"Very well then," she smiled as she gracefully sat tight to Kylie's side and took her hand, "what brings you to our door, making such a fuss?"

"Well, you see, Miss West, Sally here is the psychic on our team, and she has been having this premonition that Kylie was in danger. I'm sorry about all the fuss. The psychic thing isn't a precise science."

"Well, Sally might be right," Ella replied with a sly grin. "Kylie is in danger of suffering an attack, but I promise she will survive." She put her arm around Kylie's shoulders and hugged her tightly as she spoke.

"Stop it, Ella. Dear god, you're embarrassing. Behave yourself."

"Yes dear." Ella grinned as she released Kylie again. "But you did say you wanted to team up with me."

"Are you always so embarrassing?"

"Yes I am, so get accustomed to it."

Amanda sighed as she rose from her chair. "I think we've imposed enough for one evening. Sally, we need to talk."

"Ella, you can trust them," whispered Kylie.

"You've asked a great deal of me already, Kylie, now you ask so very much more."

"Please, you can trust them. Sally will never let it go until you do, please? I swear I will do everything in my power to protect you if..."

Ella's deep sigh stopped her cold. "Alright, Kylie, I'll do this for you. Do not make me regret it."

"*Hear me,*" Kylie shrank away, but was held in place by Ella's arm. "*Recall our first encounter.*"

There was confusion on several faces and then the terror set in. "*Obey me. From this moment forth, you will all feel comfortable and safe in my company.*" The terror faded and everyone began to relax.

"People, I want you to meet the newest member of the team, Miss Ella West, vampire hunter supreme."

"I don't understand..."

"I will explain, Agent Sawchuk," Ella smiled reassuringly. Once again she gave an account of her life, explaining what it was they were stalking, why they had not been able to kill it, and why she had to.

"So, you're the original?"

"Yes."

"But, a saber-toothed tiger? I thought vampires were made from the bite of a bat..."

"Damn that Bram Stoker anyway. If I could get my hands... no, Agent Sawchuk, I was not bitten by a bat, not ever in all my long life. I was bitten by the sabre-tooth, I hunt at night because I'm nocturnal, I can, and do walk about in the sunlight, but I don't like it. I, and I alone, can fully become the great beast, the others can only partially change. That is what killed your friends and why you couldn't kill it. That's what we must find. When we do, I'll destroy it utterly."

"So you want us to help you with the hunt?"

"We'll help each other," said Kylie. "You can trust Ella. We can't deal with that thing, and she can. We need her, and she needs our help to find it. Come on, Agent Sawchuk, old buddy, just for me, what do you say?"

"I guess you're right, Kylie. I'd really like to bring that thing down. So how am I supposed to show her on the books?"

"Miss Ella West, independent consultant," smiled Amanda. "That should work."

"Okay, I'm game," he sighed. "Welcome aboard, Miss West. How about we meet first thing tomorrow to get started?"

"I would prefer to begin tomorrow evening, as I often sleep the day away, besides, our quarry is nocturnal as well."

"Fine," Agent Sawchuck nodded. "Okay folks, it looks like we're on the night shift. Are you staying here, Kylie?"

"Yes she is. Kylie and I will arrive together," purred Ella.

"You're awful, you know that," laughed Kylie. "The only danger I'm in is dying of embarrassment."

The Hunt Begins

The next evening came and they prepared to leave the apartment. "I do wish we didn't have to go," sighed Kylie.

"And I as well; however, first we have work to do. We have delayed too long already, and the trail grows cold."

"I suppose, but it would be a lot more fun to stay put and listen to you compliment me all night."

"I promise I'll do just that one day soon, my shameless one, but first we have to find Mobutu and make an end of him."

"Can you truly kill that thing, Ella?"

"Just point him out and watch me work," she replied with a half snarl. "Come, Kylie, let us be about the task."

THEY WERE NEAR THE address where the mobile lab was located when Ella suddenly sat upright, sniffing at the air. Kylie was driving Ella's convertible with the top down, thoroughly enjoying the rush of air and the glorious woman in the passenger's seat. Startled at Ella's sudden reaction, Kylie nearly crashed the car.

"Stop the car," shouted Ella as she flung the door open. Kyle had barely slowed down when Ella leaped to the street and ran back. Slowly she returned to the spot where Kylie had double parked, muttering to herself.

"Ella, what happened?" asked Kylie, as Ella sank back into the plush leather seat.

"Mobutu was here, but the scent was old. Ah well, at least we know he's still in the city. Shall we get on with the day?"

"Sure. Ella, can I ask a favor?"

"Of course, Kylie, what do you need from me?"

"I need you to stop scaring the crap out of me, that's what I need. Dammit, woman, my startle response can't take much more."

Ella was laughing now. "Kylie, my darling, you're going to have to toughen up a bit. I'm quite old and set in my ways you know." Kylie was still giggling as they parked beside the van.

"Well, you two seem to be having a good time," commented Amanda, as they climbed into the van.

"We're off to a good start," replied Kylie.

All their smiles faded as Ella went serious. "Have you any new information as to the whereabouts of Mobutu?"

"None, but with your help, Miss West, perhaps we can get a fix on him," said Clyde.

"Please, we are colleagues now, please call me Ella."

"Tell us all you can of this man, Ella," said Amanda. "The more information we have, the better our chances."

"Mobutu is a maddened creature. He was created about five thousand years ago at best guess, and is the oldest living vampire next to me. Unlike me and those of my line, he cannot control the killing lust once it takes him. Oh, he can for a time, and he'll go as long as possible without feeding, but when the killing lust overtakes him, he loses all control. Had I not interfered that night he would have slain all of you just to hear you scream.

"About two thousand years ago I tried to destroy him, for he had deliberately invaded my territory. In the end I drove him into Africa, where he has remained much of the time since. Sadly, I believe he has played a role in much of the recent madness there. I know little of his likes or dislikes, except that he enjoys the killing, and he hates me.

"Mobutu has been wounded, and is lying low as he recovers his full strength. The problem now is that I've lost the element of surprise. Somehow he located me and came here to challenge me once again. He believed himself strong enough to defeat me, but now he knows better. He's lying low now, lulling me into a sense of security before he strikes again. The next time he'll strike from hiding and I won't have time to transform to the great cat."

"Can you defeat him, Ella?" asked Clyde.

"Under normal circumstances it would be fairly easy. As a vampire ages she grows stronger. Each time she returns from the dead she is stronger. Since I'm of such a vast age compared to Mobutu there's no question, but in this era of long distance weapons, who knows?"

"Ella...?"

"Be at peace, Kylie, I'm not dead yet," she smiled reassuringly. "We must be wary, but we will defeat him. Do not fear."

"If he knows you're so much stronger, why did he come after you?" asked Amanda.

"Mobutu believes we're gods, and he wants to be the only one. I've confined him for centuries. Each time he tries to leave Africa I kill him and send the bones back there. He revives to find himself back in the Congo every time, and it's driving him to even greater madness. This time I'll make a permanent end of him."

"Ella, what's likely to happen if he...?"

"If he defeats me, Agent Sawchuk? Should Mobutu succeed he would probably attempt to enslave all humanity into feeding herds. He'd create more like himself just to watch them attack humans."

"Do you have anything at all that he has touched or worn?" Sally asked softly.

"Ah, my little psychic friend, I thought you might have a use for this." She smiled as she pulled a small piece of cloth from her pocket and passed it to Sally.

Sally tentatively reached for the cloth, almost afraid to touch Ella's hand. "Do not fear me so, Sally. I will bring no harm to you."

"Yes you will," replied Sally, her voice a bit unsteady. "It's what you do; it's what you are. You can't deny your nature."

"No, I don't deny my nature, girl, but you do deny yours."

"Excuse me?"

"You abhor violence and aggression, yet you are a member of a very aggressive and violent species. You're protective of your friends and you fear that which I am only because you can feel my energy but you cannot read my mind, or see clearly into my heart. Stop hiding from your true self and allow the gift to take you. Release yourself to the knowledge it brings you. Become what you truly are."

Sally shrank away from the fire in Ella's eyes, but Ella turned away to Kylie. Sally stared at her back for a long moment, then defiantly sat down and began to breathe deeply, the small piece of cloth lying loosely on her lap. A few moments later she screamed and leaped to her feet as she tried to shake off the vision.

"Gods, you were right, Miss West, I mean Ella. That thing is one sick puppy."

"Did you get a fix on him, Sal?"

Sally sighed as she sank back into her chair. "He's back at the embassy, Kylie. You were right, Ella, the gift does frighten me. I have never dared to completely release myself to it like that before." She was trembling and Amanda put her arms around the girl to sooth her.

"What did you see, Sally?"

"It is too terrible to describe. I wish to God I had never seen it. It'll haunt my dreams for the rest of my life."

"It will not," Ella smiled gently. "*Hear me, Sally, you are at peace. You had a vision of a man sitting in a chair at the embassy, nothing more. You will forget all else that you have seen in that vision.*"

"Gods, it is weird the way you do that," sighed Sally as she relaxed completely. "Honestly, all I can remember is a man sitting in a chair."

"What did he look like, Sally?"

"Tall, thin, black, a big scar on his right cheek, and he had a cane right at his hand. That's him, isn't it?"

"That sounds like Mobutu. I gave him that scar at our first meeting. Funny how he always keeps that whenever he heals his body. Ah well, we have his location now and the dawn is nearly here. Take me home, Kylie. You can pick up your car from there in the morning."

"Pick up my car?"

"We know where he is now. The others can watch for him during the day, and we can watch for him at night."

"Okay, so why do I need my car?"

"I'm not trying to get rid of you, girl. I just thought it would be better if we took up different vantage points."

"Forget that, my old darling, I'm not letting you out of my sight. The Team will have plenty of surveillance on him, don't worry."

"Just you watch the age jokes, Missy. We pensioners are quite sensitive about these things."

"I'll keep that in mind," grinned Kylie as she took Ella's arm. "Here, let me help you to the door."

"For the love of mercy, can't any of you make her behave?" whined Ella, as Kylie escorted her to the door. They were still chuckling as the two women drove away.

"Ella, thanks for that," said Kylie, as she sped through the streets at the wheel of Ella's car.

"For what, honey?"

"For letting me tease you and for putting everybody at ease. I mean, you made Sally relax and all, but you were really working the room to help them relax and trust you. I want you to know how much I appreciate the effort."

"I do want them to like me, Kylie. Life is quite meaningless without friends and family, and the joys of life are so greatly enhanced when shared with someone close. I've been a bit too reclusive over the past number of years."

"Because you trusted the wrong people last time?"

"Yes indeed."

"Shall I act as a buffer for you?"

"Excuse me?"

"If I get a bad vibe about something or someone..."

"That's a wonderful idea, Kylie, thank you. I'd greatly appreciate you being a bit of a buffer for me."

"So, you're starting to trust me?"

"Yes I am, and well you know it." Ella smiled as she reached over to give Kylie's arm a gentle squeeze. "Again I thank you for the solution to the problem." Just then the phone rang, and Kylie answered. It was Sally calling for Ella. Kylie passed over the cell phone just as they reached Ella's garage.

"Ella, it's Sally. I just had a powerful impression and thought I should call. Something or someone from your far past is about to resurface. You should trust Kylie's instincts; no more can I tell you."

"Thank you for the heads up, Sally. I do appreciate your insights and will take the warning to heart. Sleep well my friend.

"Sally says something from my past is about to surface," she said as they approached the elevator. "She says I am to trust your instincts."

"Okay, so...?"

"So, if that damned phone rings, or the alarms sound, you're getting it."

"Gee thanks, Sal," grinned Kylie. As they entered the apartment the phone was ringing.

MOBUTU SAT BROODING in the huge office he occupied. He had failed again and for weeks he had been trying to come up with a way to get back the element of surprise. She'd nearly had him again. Trembling with mixed fear and rage, Mobutu glared into the mirror across the room. He ran his finger along the scar she had given him at their first meeting. Mobutu kept the scar as a reminder to always be on guard. She was horribly fast and strong.

Gazing at the scar made him angry and the rage began to overpower the fear. She should have been finished. If that damned fool of an Englishman had just done what he was told... He should have killed the lot of them that night and burned the place down around them, disposing of the head himself. He began to pound on the steel desk in frustration.

One of his henchmen came to see what was happening. "Boss?"

"Have you located that bitch yet?"

"No sir, we can't find her anywhere."

With a scream of primal rage Mobutu leaped on the hapless man, driving long fangs deep into his neck. The man struggled for a moment then lay dead in Mobutu's hands. He cast the body aside and licked his lips as several more of his henchmen entered the office with guns drawn. They froze at the sight of their companion's mangled body.

"Get out there and find her, now. Find the hag or the same fate awaits you all." His men fled the outer office. They could still hear him raving as they reached the parking lot.

Harald the Saxon

Kylie put the phone on speaker. "West residence, Kylie Green speaking."

"This is Robert Essex speaking. Is this the residence of Miss Ella West, an emigrant from England?"

Kylie's smile faded as she saw Ella's reaction to the man's voice. "Yes sir, it is."

"May I speak with Miss West please?" he asked, impatience beginning to show in his voice.

"May I ask the nature of your call, Mr. Essex?"

"Just ask her if she recognizes the name, Harald Eldredsson?"

"What do you want, Harald?" Ella demanded in a no-nonsense voice as she approached the phone.

"Actually, it's Robert now, Mother."

"I'm not your mother, Harald."

"Yes, well, close enough. Listen, I didn't call to start a fight, and before you ask, I'm not in your territory; I'm still at home in London. Why I should bother explaining that bit is beyond me, as you managed to waltz through my territory without so much as a by your leave."

"Is he always this sweet?" asked Kylie.

"Not really, dear. Harald is on best behavior today."

"Yes, yes, have your fun, Ella, but we must talk in private. This is important and you will want to hear it."

111

"You may speak freely in front of Kylie, Robert is it? Kylie is very much aware of me and some of my history."

"Only some?"

"Well, I do go back a long way. It would take a while to tell it all."

"Indeed, well, no sense boring your paramour to death, is there?"

"Harald, for the love of mercy will you get to the point? Why have you called?"

"Right, sorry. Including you, Mother dear, there are exactly eight of us alive to tell the tale."

"Only eight including me?"

"Mobutu has left Africa. He stopped off in Italy long enough to kill Gina. You last knew her as Illona. She's been utterly destroyed and will not return, or so the message he left on the body said. Where he went from there we don't know for certain, for we can't find him."

"He's here in New York, Robert, we hunt each other even now. I had him in my claws, but the cursed weasel wriggled free and escaped me. It will not happen again. Did you mean to say you are all looking for him?"

"Yes. This is the information age, and we can now stay in touch without actually entering each other's territory. We have also formed an alliance for mutual protection. I do have to confess, I was quite relieved, and actually a bit thrilled, to catch your scent on the streets of London. I looked, but you had already gone."

"I do beg pardon, Robert, I wasn't aware that you'd left Berlin for London, or I surely would have been more polite. So you have formed an alliance, and you've called to tell me this because..."

"We all want you to join us."

"All?"

"All. Nothing can be done without full consensus; this is how the alliance works. We keep each other informed as to our travels, and territories. We share wealth if necessary, help obtain new identities, etc. and we're determined to face all threats with a united front. We're not trying to overcome our nature, but in this age of intrusion, we need each other if we're to survive. You're the one who created us all. Will you not lead us now?"

"Lead you?"

"Join with us. Give us the benefit of your experience, help us to survive as you did once before, that sort of thing."

"Har... Robert, I confess I'm somewhat taken aback here." Ella sank into her chair. "Tell me all of it now. Stop dragging it out."

"Alright, Mother..."

"Ella, if you please, Robert. Don't push your luck..."

"Yes, Ella. Sorry, but you really must change your name once in a while you know. Yes, yes, the full story. Well, about forty years ago there was this idiot of a catholic monk who thought he was the reincarnation of the fictitious Van Helsing. He was quite mad, but he nearly did manage to make an end of Natasha. It was pure luck that Gina happened on them and drank the bugger dry.

"Anyway, the girls made a pact to keep in touch, and to offer mutual assistance if needed. It proved beneficial, and eventually we were all drawn in. Normally we remain far apart as always, but when Gina called, well, we heard her final screams over the cell phone. We're all gathered here in London now..."

"All of you? In one place?"

"You taught us to overcome the killing lust, so we felt the natural aversion to sharing space could be overcome in times of emergency as well. We're pleased to say it's working, although I will admit we get on each other's nerves a bit."

"Now I'm in shock."

"I see you have not lost your flair for the dramatic, Mother," chuckled a deep voice.

"Peter? You two are actually in the same room?"

"Conference call, Mother dear," purred a soft feminine voice. "For the sake of all our sanity, we're in separate hotel rooms. You really do need to catch up on the possibilities of the technology a bit."

"I can see that. So, you can share territory for a time, you give aid where needed, share information, etc. Is that it?"

"In a nutshell," replied Robert. "It's nothing too formal, but its purpose is mutual survival above all else. That brings me to the second reason for my call. We'd like your permission to send someone to New York to assist you in dealing with Mobutu. We had planned to beg you to come here, but if he's there, then that's where we should be."

"You all want to help me?"

"Yes. You made it possible for each of us to survive, so, in effect, you are our mother, and we wish to help you. Mobutu will kill us all one by one if he can. Only together can we defeat him. He's too old and strong for any single one of us. When you disappeared for so long we were afraid he had made good his boast. He believes that you fear him and so he went hunting for you."

"Yes, well, I disabused him of that silly notion a few days past. The dirty sod escaped me then, but I'll find him again, and I will make an end of him." She looked to Kylie who was nodding her head that Ella should agree. "Very well, I'll accept your terms of association, and I'll accept any and all of you in my territory as long as you warn me you're coming."

"How many do you need for this hunt?"

"I have Kylie with me for the hunt. Kylie's human, but she is by far the best urban tracker there is, and she is immune to the compulsion."

"Immune?" exclaimed several voices. "And she yet lives?"

"She does, and she will continue to do so, or I will be extremely vexed, do I make myself clear?"

"Very clear, Ella," came another voice, "but the risk..."

"Please people," said Kylie softly. "I swear your secret is safe with me. I'm a friend here."

"Prey and predator do not often make friends, girl," came the deep male voice.

"No sir, not often, but in my own way I'm a hunter too, so I do have a basic understanding of the issues."

"Ah well, brothers and sisters," sighed Robert, "we've asked Mother to take a leap of faith for us. It's only just that we do the same for her. Agreed?"

"Agreed," replied several voices with varying degrees of enthusiasm.

"Very good then, Mother, how many do you need?"

"Only one or two. Hear me, I can deal with Mobutu, but I need Kylie to track him, and it would be helpful if she had a bodyguard or two with special talents. Remember, she is not to be harmed."

"We live by the code you taught us, Ella. Harm no innocents, stalk the predators, feed only as necessary, and leave no unexplained bodies behind. The woman is safe. She will not be harmed," replied Robert. "I'm the eldest, and therefore the strongest. I'll come."

"As will I," agreed the soft feminine voice, "with your permission of course, Ella. Robert is indeed the strongest, but I have by far the most combat experience."

"Still working as a mercenary, Helga?"

"It is Gudrun now, Mother, and yes, it keeps me on the night shift."

"You have my permission to come, and thank you all. Listen people, I have to say that I applaud what you all have managed to do, for I was thinking along the same lines just recently. I was considering seeking you out to test the idea, when that idiot Mobutu showed up and started killing everyone in sight. If the humans ever discover what he is, they'll hunt us all into extinction. I agree that we do need to band together for mutual benefit."

"Wonderful, we shall contact you when we arrive."

"I'll set the phone to forward calls to my cell, so you can reach me at any time of day or night."

"Thank you, Mother. See you soon."

"It truly was good to hear from you all this way. Good night, my children."

Ella sat staring at the phone for a long moment, a strange look on her face. "Ella, are you alright? Is everything okay?" Kylie asked tentatively.

"A few weeks ago my life was fully under control, well ordered, and I felt sure in my domain, secure in my place in the world, and how to maintain it."

"And now?"

"And now it has all gone to hell in a hand basket. What have I done to myself? Gods, I should just vanish for a hundred years or so."

"Ella, please don't do that."

"Peace, Kylie, I'm just whining. I had Mobutu in my sights, but a human girl charged him first. He was killing your friends, and you went rushing in. I'd intended to let him finish the lot of you and take him as he fed, while his guard was down, but..."

"You charged in to save me?"

"It seemed like the right idea at the time. He saw me coming and put you between us for just a heartbeat, but it was enough to allow his escape. I couldn't get a tight grip on him in time."

"That's why you were so angry with me. I made you miss."

"My anger was merely frustration, nothing more, Kylie."

"Ella, talk to me."

"Alright, Kylie. Normally I would just have charged over you and taken him down, but, for some reason, I changed course enough to miss you. He saw the move and it was enough."

"Why?"

"More than once I have brought down a great stag, and taken only what I needed to survive. I let them live because they didn't flee from me leaving their herd at the mercy of the predator. They put themselves in my path to allow the herd a chance to escape. Such courage should be allowed to pass to the next generation."

"You admire courage, don't you, Ella."

"I do."

"And that's why you lost the killer this time. You deliberately avoided hurting me."

"Yes, that is so."

"I swear I'll try to be worthy of that gift, Ella. I'll hold all your secrets sacred, and take them with me to the grave."

"Thank you, Kylie, but I do hope you'll keep them warm for another eighty years or so. I'm quite enjoying your company. Alas, it's now time to rely on another, something I have not done since I was driven from my clan as a young woman."

"You were driven out?"

"I was a mutant even before the great cat remade me, Kylie. I grew too fast and too strong for the others. None would mate with me, and I was driven out. I've relied on myself alone ever since that day."

"But now?"

"But now I'm going to trust you and your friends. Give me your thoughts on what just happened here tonight."

"Well, it seems that you did have children after all. Although you're quite solitary by nature, they've banded together for mutual benefit, and they've asked you to lead them. It feels right to me, Ella. The way technology is advancing, it'll soon become impossible for any of you to remain hidden without assistance."

"What do you recommend we do, Kylie?"

"Somehow you all must develop a network of humans who will help you. You also must become masters of modern technology. The more you're able to understand it, the better you'll be able to defend yourselves, and manipulate it to your own advantage."

"So, will you help me attain this mastery?"

"Yes, my immortal love, I'll help you, but we need Tommy, and for some reason he just up and quit. Amanda's been working on him, and says he might return. I hope he does, Tommy's a wizard with technology."

"Immortal? Yes, I suppose that's what I am."

"I like the sound of that much better than 'vampire.' From now on I will refer to you all as immortals."

"I like it, Kylie, I do like it. Now then, we'll have a busy night coming up, so we'd better get some rest."

"Aren't you going hunting?"

"No, Kylie, it'll be many days now before I need to hunt again, besides, it's too near dawn. Today we rest."

"Okay, so..."

"The bedroom is this way, as you well know," grinned Ella, as she began to undress and drop her clothes on the floor as she headed to the bedroom. "You may sleep where you choose, Kylie. I'll be in here, and there's plenty of room. You have been hinting, after all."

"Just be gentle with me," grinned Kylie as she followed Ella.

Ella turned and took Kylie into her arms gently. "I will not ever hurt you, Kylie. I swear I won't, and I swear I'll strive to be worthy of the courage you show in trusting me. Come now, all is well."

Ella's soft breath teased the nape of Kylie's neck, sending small shivers of delight through her as she melted into her immortal's embrace. Gentle hands loosened and removed her clothing as soft lips caressed their way down her throat and to her breast. She gasped again as she felt Ella's fangs slowly extend, brushing along her nipple then retract again.

Kylie was scooped up easily and her naked body laid gently on the bed. She gasped in fear and delight as she saw the look of pure lust on Ella's face. With the grace of a stalking cat, Ella climbed onto the bed to hover over Kylie's prone body, her head lowering as she sought a kiss. Her tongue was strangely rough as she and Kylie kissed passionately.

The girl's breath was coming in ragged gasps now as those soft lips made their way slowly down her body. She began to moan softly as gentle hands slipped beneath her knees, lifting her legs into the air where those hungry lips found her thighs.

Kylie was raised to levels of arousal she had never known before, as the fear and desire took her and drove her on to ecstasy. Dawn arrived to find her fast asleep in the arms of an immortal, a smile of pure delight on her face.

Return of the Cat

"So, anything new?" asked Kylie, as she and Ella entered the mobile lab.

"Something is sure new with you," observed Sally. Kylie stuck out her tongue at Sally then turned to Agent Sawchuk who was peering at a computer screen.

"Something weird's going on," mused Sawchuk. "Something sure has our friend agitated. We've been listening to him rant for hours, but we can't figure out a single word he says. That language isn't in our recognition database. Sure wish I knew what he was up to."

Ella turned her attention to the agent. "Have you recorded what he has said?"

"Yes I did." The gentle voice belonged to Tommy. He was a slim and somewhat timid looking man. In truth that is exactly what he was. Tommy had managed to survive the bullying at school and go on to become a brilliant electrical engineer.

"I see you've returned, Tommy. They said you'd quit. Is this true?"

"Yes. I just had this overpowering panic attack. I don't have any idea what the threat was, but after seeing that thing kill Leon and Mendez, I just cracked I guess. So tell me, just who are you, and how come you seem to know me when we have never met before?"

"We have met before, Tommy."

"No Ma'am, I'd surely remember you if we had."

"Kylie?"

"You can trust Tommy, sweetheart, and we do need him," replied Kylie, still gazing over Agent Sawchuk's shoulder.

"Tommy, my name is Ella West."

"A real pleasure to meet you, Miss West. Can you tell me where we are supposed to have met before?"

"*Tommy, recall our first encounter,*" commanded Ella in that terrible voice that sent shivers through them all.

"Oh Jesus," gasped Tommy as he began to back away from her.

"*Be at peace, Tommy. You will always feel safe in my company from this moment forward.*"

Bemused, Tommy began to visibly relax. "Thanks for that. I know I shouldn't trust it, but for some reason, I do."

"Do you trust Sally's insights, Tommy?" Kylie asked.

"Absolutely."

"Sally trusts me, Tommy."

"Did you make her do it?"

"Yes I did," laughed Ella. "Very well, let's get this settled right now." She took a step towards Sally causing her to flinch involuntarily. To Sally's great surprise Ella sank to the floor at her feet. "Now, Sally, what do you need from me to get a clear reading?"

"Can I touch something of yours?"

"Anything at all, except Kylie." This brought a round of laughter from the others and a blush to Kylie's face. "Here, Sally, take my hands. Do what you must now."

Tentatively, Sally took Ella's hands then closed her eyes and drew several deep gentle breaths. She was silent for a few moments, but she was visibly relaxing. "You're old beyond imagining, but you're also young. Life still holds magic for you. You dislike bullies, because you were bullied then driven away, and so you only feed from the violent of our species. You would prefer to hunt horses or other wild game, but instead you hunt aggressive humans.

"You have children, but almost never see them. You've been killed a few times, but you always return stronger than before. You're quite protective of those you love, and you're deadly to your enemies.

"You have a tendency to trust too easily, and that has caused you much heartbreak in the past, therefore you're now having trouble allowing yourself to trust at all. You are as afraid of us as we are of you, but for different reasons.

"Kylie is the beginning of great change for you. She's the catalyst that will take your long life in new and different directions. Kylie will defend you every bit as rigorously as you will defend her and all of us.

"Grave danger stalks you both, but help is drawing nearer even now. It will be difficult, but you must trust your children, as well as Kylie's instincts. You also know you should kill me, as my talent could pose a great threat to you, but you won't harm me."

Slowly Sally's eyes opened and she gently squeezed the hands in her own. "You really won't hurt me, will you, Ella?"

"I have promised that I won't, Sally, and I'll keep my word. I will not harm you. Tell the others what you've learned now."

"Ella's a vampire, no question, but she's not driven by the blood lust, she controls it. We have to help her; our streets are far safer with her here than they are without her."

"Are you satisfied now, Tommy?"

"Yes, Miss West, but can I ask you something?"

"Of course."

"If you need our help, why not just make us do it?"

"I don't enjoy controlling others, Tommy. It's too easy to rely on that. I like to have my wits about me all the time, and I need my friends to be the same. I don't want to control you all. I want us to work together, so please call me Ella."

"That works for me, Ella," sighed Tommy. "Here's some of what we recorded." Suddenly the lab was filled with the sounds of a madman ranting. Sally cringed at that voice, but Ella tucked Sally under her arm, and suddenly Sally knew for certain she was safe with the vampire, at least this one.

"That's enough, Tommy," Ella suddenly declared. "Can we take this unit to the airport?"

"Sure," replied Agent Sawchuk. "Why?"

"We have allies about to arrive. Mobutu is aware of them, how I do not know. Somehow he must have been watching me, or has tapped my phone. He intends to intercept them, and I'd like to intercept him first."

"The car will be faster," declared Kylie as she strode to the door. "You guys bring the van. Come on, sugar, let's go hunting."

"He's on the move," shouted Agent Sawchuk. "He's moving away from the embassy." Ella and Kylie were already gone.

The car raced through the streets, Ella continuing to test the air. "He's ahead of us somewhere, faster Kylie, faster."

"I can't unless I put up a siren."

"Do your best, my love. Don't allow my impatience to cloud your judgment."

"Ella, he's heading out of the city. What's going on here? The airport is the other way."

"Indeed. Kylie, I suspect we have a spy in our midst."

"What?"

"How else could he be aware of our impending guest's arrival, and why did he suddenly change his mind about intercepting them?"

"Somehow he's getting information. That means he knows about the team, and he knows where we live. Ella, we didn't decide to meet the airplane personally until just a few minutes ago and you were there with us."

"So he was listening to us even as we were listening to him?"

"Crap. Here's my cell, Agent Sawchuk is #3 on the speed dial. Call him and tell him what is going on. Somehow that bastard has bugged the van or something."

Ella dialed and relayed the message to Agent Sawchuk. "Alright, Ella, stay on him, maybe we'll get lucky. Tommy will sweep the van for bugs, and I'll sweep the area for listening posts. Stay in touch."

Ella sighed as she closed the phone. They were leaving the city now and Kylie was making better speed. She turned off the headlights as she spoke. "None of the team betrayed us, Ella, I'd bet my life on it. In fact, I guess I already have, haven't I?"

"No, you have not, and I'm getting a bit annoyed at the lot of you going about as though you expect me to leap on you and rip out your throat at any moment. Kylie, you and the team are completely safe from me, I swear it. If it turns out we have a traitor, you get to deal with it. Will that satisfy you?"

"Ella, please forgive me. There's a lot of pop culture about vampires that I'm still trying to overcome here. Give us a bit of time."

"Forgive me, Kylie. Can I ask you a question?"

"Sure lover."

"Why did you bother turning off the lights? Won't the driving lights still be visible?"

"Aw crap, this is your car. I disabled the driving lights in mine. Okay, I guess I have to do this the hard way." She eased off the accelerator with a deep sigh. "Can you still smell him?"

"Yes, we're still on the right road. Wait, the scent is growing fainter; it's gone."

"He must have turned off on that last intersection. Hang on." She pulled a swift maneuver and the car was suddenly facing the other way.

"Nice, but if he was still within miles he would have heard the squeal of the tires."

"Ella honey, are we still okay?" sighed Kylie as she reached the right turning.

"Yes love, we are. Sorry to let my impatience show so easily."

"And I'm sorry that I keep overlooking the obvious."

"Kylie?"

"I'm not tracking a human; I'm tracking an animal. This quarry has much keener senses than the ones I'm used to. What else do I need to know?"

"He hears as well as any dog, sees in the dark like a cat, is faster, stronger, and more deadly than any lion, and he is as crafty as they come. His survival instincts are extremely keen." At this point the phone rang and Ella answered. It was Agent Sawchuk.

"You were right, Miss West, he had a spy, but it wasn't one of us. We found a bug on the van and a listening post nearby. We got the guys at the listening post, but I have bad news. They're members of an organized crime gang. Our killer is tapped into some serious shit here, and I'm willing to bet he has a lot of help. We'll continue to work it from this end, and Tommy'll debug your phone line at the apartment. Good hunting." Ella sighed and relayed the information to Kylie, as she turned up a side road toward a wooded area.

"The scent is stronger now," Ella declared as they came out of the trees and into an area of farmland. "He's nearby. That way."

Kylie dutifully turned up the smaller road. It led them to a fenced compound. The heavy gate was padlocked from the inside, and the fence was over ten feet high. "Well, it looks like he's gone to ground," mused Kylie as she turned off the engine, effectively cutting the lights at last. "Got any bolt cutters in the trunk?"

"He is near," snarled Ella as she leaped from the car.

"Get down!" hissed Kylie, trying to move Ella behind a tree.

"Kylie, what is it?"

"Have you ever heard of a gun? You said this guy is crafty. If I wanted to take out an immortal, I'd certainly use a gun to slow her down, weaken her a bit."

Ella turned and pulled Kylie gently into her arms. "That's good thinking, Kylie. That's just the type of thing he'd do. I'm willing to bet that's now the plan he's hatching. He's lured me out to this place in hopes of just such an opportunity."

"So, what do we do now?"

"The average bullet will certainly give me pause, but not my friend. Unless he has an elephant gun in there, the cat will bring him down."

"Ella, he knows what you are. He probably does have an elephant gun in there, maybe more. We should be careful here. We need to call in reinforcements, check out the lay of the land..."

"Good idea, sweetheart, you call for backup while I check out the terrain."

She was already stripping off her clothes as she spoke and Kylie's protest died on her lips as Ella shimmered into the great cat. Kylie involuntarily shrank away from the rippling mass of muscle, as a silent snarl crossed the cat's face. Their eyes met for a moment then the cat stepped closer and rubbed against Kylie's side. Hesitantly Kylie stroked the soft fur then stepped away as the great beast crouched and tensed every muscle in that gigantic body. With a single bound it was over the fence.

Kylie was astounded at how easily the massive cat blended into the background. As Ella moved closer to the buildings an alarm was triggered. At the sound of the alarm the cat flattened itself to the ground. Both she and the cat heard the baying as the guard dogs were released.

With a roar of protest the cat turned back toward the fence, but the dogs were already on her. Under normal circumstances the dogs would have prevailed easily, but not this time. These were oversized and savage dogs, but still no match for a saber-toothed tiger. Kylie watched in horror as the pack attacked and met their fate. Even with all their strength and speed, it was over swiftly. Five dead mastiffs and one in the jaws of the cat as she drank deeply, renewing her strength.

Her thirst quenched; the cat roared again. Snarling her frustration she started towards the buildings once more, but a car suddenly sped away through another gate. She could not follow; several shots rang out, the bullets spraying up dirt around her. The great cat turned, and with a leap that defied gravity, she cleared the fence once again. Kylie already had the car turned around by the time Ella was herself again. She struggled into her clothes while the car raced back towards the city, unable to catch the quarry.

"I'll head straight for the airport," Kylie declared as she took a tight turn. "That's probably where he's going."

"It's alright, sweetheart, take your time and get us there in one piece. He's slipped through our fingers once again. I'm starting to get tired of letting Mobutu lead the dance. We need a plan to lure him into our choice of terrain."

"Agreed, my love, but right now we need to make sure our guests arrive in good order. Once they're safely on the ground I'm going to find this bugger, he's really starting to piss me off."

"Forgive me, Kylie, but that is such a vulgar expression. Could you choose another?"

"He's starting to annoy me greatly?"

"Much better and thank you."

"Anything for my kitten."

"Kitten? Are you calling me a kitten?"

"Well, I did have you purring yesterday."

"If you're trying to distract me, Kylie, you're doing a fine job," chuckled Ella. "However, we need to see our guests into a secure hotel before I can take you home."

"Will you need to hunt, Ella?"

"No dear, the dog was quite sufficient. My oath, what magnificent animals, but there was some of Mobutu's madness about them. I wonder if he..."

"No Ella, those babies were specially bred by the drug gangs, to guard the stash. They'll attack anything that moves, and kill or be killed is all they do. They're intended to keep the police at bay."

"Indeed, well their strength and courage is now mine, and I feel wonderful. It's been many long years since I fed from such a beast. Remind me to thank Mobutu once I've destroyed him."

"Yes dear," laughed Kylie as she negotiated another turn. They could see the lights of the airport in the distance.

SALLY TRIED TO RELAX in the back of the swaying van as it raced toward the airport. Suddenly she sat up and screamed. She'd had a vision of her Viking again; she'd seen him fall and heard the gunshot.

Guests

The airport was no different than any other, and the two travelers aroused no extra attention. They cleared customs and headed for the baggage area. They were almost to the carousel when a shot rang out. The man clutched his chest and sank towards the floor. "For god's sake, play dead," hissed his companion as he fell.

The woman had seen the flash of the gun barrel, and was after the shooter in a heartbeat. Cursing to herself as she held her speed down, she nonetheless sent him running in terror. She chased him right into the waiting arms of airport security.

As soon as they had him she returned to her fallen companion. A paramedic was just zipping the body bag as she reached them. "Ma'am, I'm so very sorry for your loss, but we couldn't save him. We tried everything, but by the size of the hole, the shooter must have used ..."

"I'll take charge of that, young man," announced a short powerfully built man who flashed some kind of badge. "My name is Agent Sawchuk, and I'll be handling the investigation. You there, is there a secure room we can use?"

"Yes sir," replied a uniformed security officer, "right through this door."

"Very good. Bring the body inside and send the police to me as soon as they arrive. Ma'am, if you would be so kind as to accompany me..."

He indicated that the tall woman should enter the room as well. With a half knowing smile she preceded him into the secure room. Several others followed them in and closed the door. "Agent Sawchuk, at your service ma'am," he grinned as the door closed. "You would be the folks Ella West was expecting?"

"Indeed so, Agent Sawchuk. So, you're the welcoming committee?"

"We knew Mobutu wanted to intercept you, but for some reason he broke and ran. Ella and Kylie are on his trail right now. We came on ahead, hoping to get set up before your plane arrived, but we were too late."

"I know."

"Yes, well, is there anything special he'll need when he wakes up?"

"You know what we are?"

"We do. Tell me what we need, and I'll make arrangements to get you out of here below the radar."

"We must get him out unseen, and he'll need to feed soon. He's not asleep, just playing dead while he heals the wound. He can last a while yet, but not all that long. Speed is of the essence. And my name is Gudrun."

"Yes Miss Gudrun, I heard that," grinned Agent Sawchuk as he opened his cell phone and began to dial. The tall blonde woman watched approvingly as he made all the necessary arrangements to get her companion safely out of the busy airport.

ELLA AND KYLIE ARRIVED to find a serious commotion going on. They were stopped by the police, but Kylie's badge got them through. What's going on?" demanded Ella.

"A man was shot ma'am," sighed a young police officer. "He was a British national. We have the shooter in custody, but he won't talk. Your fellow agents are with the man's wife right now. They're through that door right there."

Following the young man's directions, they found the team in a secure office with a tall blonde woman. She half smiled, half snarled as she saw Ella. "Hello, Mother, it's been a long time."

"Yes it has, Gudrun is it?" replied Ella, her voice cool. "It was Robert who got shot?"

"Yes. Did you get Mobutu?"

"Alas no, he slipped through our fingers again. Where's the body?"

"He's right here, Ella. I've sent for a special ambulance," said Agent Sawchuk. "We've taken control of the body. I've also arranged for several bags of blood to be on the ambulance. I've been informed he'll be hungry very soon now."

"Yes he will. Have you taken control of the shooter as well?"

"Miss Gudrun caught him. The locals have him and are still looking for the other one. I gave them a photo of this Mobutu and told them he's a terrorist. I don't expect them to find him, but it'll keep them entertained while we question the one we have. Ah, I see they're ready to hand him over."

Tommy had assisted Clara in searching the shooter's staging area. They found nothing of great interest, so they returned to the van. Amanda and Clyde remained to help with the questioning. The two policemen half dragged a handcuffed man towards the team. "Here he is, Agent Sawchuk. Hope you have better luck than we did. These gangsters never talk."

"He'll talk to me," purred Gudrun, as she reached towards the prisoner.

"Keep your hands off, bitch, unless you want to play," snarled the tattooed man in cuffs.

She reached for him so swiftly he couldn't react. Gripping his shoulder hard enough to break bone, she forced him to his knees. "Speak only when I command you to do so. You may remove your handcuffs gentlemen. I won't need them."

Puzzled, and a bit unsure, the policeman uncuffed the prisoner then withdrew. The man tried to bolt, but Gudrun caught him easily by the throat. She was too strong, and he began to panic as, with the pressure of her thumb alone, she turned his face away to expose his throat. For only a brief moment, with her back to the others, she allowed him to see her fangs. The man wet himself and began to babble. "Don't, please don't..."

"Perhaps not," she smiled coldly as she dropped him to the floor. "Robert will be hungry when he awakens. You will now answer all Agent Sawchuk's questions truthfully. I will know if you lie, and you'll pay one pint of blood for each lie. Agent Sawchuk, perhaps we should take him somewhere quiet for the interrogation."

"Wonderful idea, Ma'am, I know just the place."

"Wait, please, I don't know nothin' about nothin'. I was just supposed to show up and pop the Brit, that's all. There was a down payment for the hit, and a picture of the mark sent to me. His hair was too dark, but the face was right, so I shot him. That's all I know."

"He's telling the truth," sighed Ella.

"Have you ever seen this man?" demanded Amanda as she showed the shooter a picture of Mobutu.

"No, no, wait, maybe. There was this guy hanging around the bars late at night, you know. Could have been him, I'm not sure."

"Perhaps I could refresh your memory..."

"When was the last time you had a proper meal, Gudrun?" asked Ella softly.

"It's been too long, several days in fact, and I'm starting to feel a bit on edge."

"Kylie honey, take her downtown to the apartment please."

"Gotcha," replied Kylie, as she nodded her head slowly to say that she fully understood. "Come on, Blondie, let's go. We'll grab a bite along the way."

Kylie led the way out with a smiling Gudrun following close on her heels. As they got in the car and started away, her passenger looked her over carefully. "Just you remember who I am. Try anything funny and Momma will be pissed."

"It's been nearly a thousand years since I was foolish enough to make her angry with me," sighed Gudrun. "We were in London at the time. When I returned from the lands beyond, I was in Siberia with a note of admonishment pinned to my chest. I've learned a lot of self discipline since that time, and I still have the note. I'll show it to you one day, Kylie. Now, talk to me. How did you and Ella get together?"

"Our team was on the trail of a serial killer. We didn't know another hunter was also tracking him. We got to him first and paid the price for it. We lost two guys and nearly lost another. I was rushing in someplace where I should never have gone, when a saber-toothed tiger tore into the killer. Unfortunately, in trying to avoid hurting me, she allowed his escape. She wasn't happy with me."

"On the contrary, my dear, she must have been quite impressed with you. You're still here aren't you? Once she realized you were immune to the compulsion..."

"I know. In truth she should have killed me the minute she found out."

"Curious, why didn't she?"

"I talked her out of it."

"Really, and how did you manage that?"

"I proposed."

"Good strategy, I'll have to remember that."

"Hey, back off, sister. Cat Woman is mine."

"I like you, Kylie Green. I think we shall be great friends."

"Just as long as you don't get too hungry."

"Speaking of that, you did promise me dinner."

"Almost there. Did I hear right? You're a mercenary soldier?"

"That's right. You know, get a job, see the world, that sort of thing. I actually enjoy the para-military life. I lead a small troop of elite forces. We do a lot of special ops. You know, in and out quickly. We never enter prolonged battles. Just accomplish our mission and get out."

"Do your troops know about...?"

"No. I could never trust them with that."

"No?"

"They're mercenaries, remember? Any one of them would sell me out in a heartbeat."

"Sounds like a dangerous line of work."

"It is, but as Mother would say, where's the thrill without the risk?"

"I've heard that more than once. Okay, here we are at the apartment," sang Kylie as she pulled over. "That lever will ring the bell. I'll be inside and let you in from there. We'll get you to a hotel after you've had a good meal. Now, I'll drop you off about three blocks away where there's always some action. Come for me when you're ready, and we'll go to the hotel from there. Remember..."

"There'll be no dead bodies this night, little sister. I swear it."

"Okay, here we are. I'll grab a pizza and wait for you back at the apartment." She waved and sped off as Gudrun closed the car door. Kylie barely had time to finish her pizza before the woman returned.

BACK AT THE AIRPORT the search proved fruitless. Ella made the shooter forget the interrogation then ordered him to confess. They had the body in the ambulance and Ella sat with it. As soon as the doors closed, Ella unzipped the body bag and let him out. He was ravenous. She gave him the three bags of blood, and that seemed to satisfy him for the moment.

"Welcome to New York, Robert," she smiled as he drained the third bag of blood.

"I need more..."

"And more you shall have, trust me. Just hang in there a few more minutes."

"All right, I can do that," sighed the dark haired man.

"I must say, Robert. I was expecting a blonde man."

"I had hoped that Mobutu was as well." A moment's focus and his hair turned golden once again. "Gudrun said it was a waste of time. Is she...?"

"She's fine, Robert. Kylie's dropped her off in my favorite hunting ground. She'll be well fed by the time we arrive."

"Your favorite hunting ground... Might I perhaps..."

"We're on our way there as we speak. My friends are arranging everything; please trust now and be patient. Tell me all you can remember of what happened."

"Well, we were stuck together the whole trip as we're traveling as a couple. Fortunately, we were in business class. If we'd been in steerage, I swear she would have eaten somebody. The flight was long and tedious, but uneventful. We passed through customs easily enough.

"As we entered the main terminal, I felt as though I had been hit by a broad sword. I saw Gudrun go after someone, and all I could do from there was play dead until I was taken to a more private place. Fortunately for me, your people were on the scene and took care of everything; otherwise the whole world would have seen me heal.

"It's funny you know, Ella. We suppress the need for blood constantly so one almost becomes unaware of it at times, but upon healing a bad injury; it's as fresh as the first time. I'd forgotten how powerful that need can be."

"Indeed so, but I must say, you're controlling it nicely. I... Ah, here we are. Outside this ambulance is a fine hunting ground. Take what you need then return to this place. The ambulance will be gone, but I and my friends will still be here. My scent will guide you." Ella suddenly took him into her arms and hugged him tightly. "Drink deeply of my scent now, Robert, and then hunt."

He did as she bid him. She released him and opened the doors. He was gone into the shadows in a heartbeat. Ella abandoned the ambulance and sought out her team in the van. It wasn't far away. "All is well?" asked Amanda as Ella entered the van.

"He's hunting," Sally said. "I can feel his need. My God, such a powerful addiction! It's much stronger than what I feel from you, Ella."

"He's newly healed from a bad injury, Sally. Robert will feed, but he'll be fine. You know, people, it occurs to me that you could do us all a great favor."

"All of us?"

"Me and my...children, shall we say."

"How can we help you, Ella?" asked Amanda.

"Actually, Amanda, it's you and Clyde who can be the most help. You see, in times past it was easy for us to remain hidden from the general public. Human kind has always had more to fear from itself than from us, for there was no need to hunt humans, but that's irrelevant now. In this age of information and invasive technology, we've become vulnerable."

"I should think Tommy would be more help than Amanda or I."

"Indeed, Tommy would be invaluable to us, and if he's willing..."

"Just don't let them bite my head off, and I'd be happy to help, Ella."

"Thank you, Tommy. You see, Clyde, we're a solitary folk by nature. We go hundreds of years without seeing another of our own kind. When we do encounter one another, it's often violent as we're quite territorial. Having said all that, the others have managed to band together for mutual protection and benefit. That's why Robert and Gudrun are here, to help us dispose of Mobutu."

"So, you're thinking we can help you all learn to overcome your natural aversion to each other," smiled Amanda.

"Yes."

"Well, count me in. The only complaint I have, is I won't be able to document the case study. Amanda?"

"I'm there, Clyde my friend, I'm there. Ella, we know we can't publish the work, but the chance to..."

"Crawl around in our heads..."

"The desire is nearly as strong as your hunger," laughed Amanda.

"Forgive me, Amanda, but that's the first time I've seen you smile or heard you laugh," Ella said gently.

"It's a long story, Ella. Perhaps I'll tell it sometime, but not right now."

"He's returning," said Sally, as she rose from her chair. "His hunger's been satisfied for the moment."

Agent Sawchuk stepped out just as Robert crossed the street. He ushered the powerfully built stranger into the mobile lab, and Ella introduced him around. "It's a pleasure to meet you all. I say, you must be the one," smiled Robert as he turned his full attention to Sally.

"What do you mean?" she asked as she backed away from him.

"It is you," he said, his smile broadening. "You're the one who's been poking around in my mind for years." Sensing her fear, he relaxed his posture completely. "Sally, is it? Come here to me, Sally. I won't harm you."

Robert held out his hands, palms up, and slowly Sally came closer and reached for his hands, her eyes never leaving his. As her hands touched his he gently pulled her closer until she was well inside his personal space. "Good, now release yourself to your feelings, your senses, and your special vision."

She hesitated for a moment then closed her eyes and drew a deep breath. "You were once a king," she breathed softly, then fell silent. They all smiled as Sally visibly relaxed further and smiled as she opened herself to the Saxon's energy. Suddenly she blushed deeply. Her eyes flew open and she thrust his hands away, her eyes wide and her mouth making a perfect 'O'. "Just you behave yourself, sir," she admonished as she stepped away from him.

"Is he always like this?" Sally demanded of Ella.

"Actually, I've never seen him like this before, Sally. I think the poor boy is besotted with you."

"Forgive me, Mother, but she is terribly distracting. I could feel her near me as I hunted. Never in all my long years has anything cut through the need like the presence of Sweet Sally. That truly helped me to stay focused. Sally, my love, you're the woman from my dreams; you have no reason at all to fear me."

"Oh yes I do," Sally replied tartly, her face still crimson, "but for very different reasons now. I know what you're like."

Everyone was laughing, and that only added to Sally's embarrassment. Just then the phone rang. "Sawchuk," he grunted as he punched the speaker button.

"Kylie here. Gudrun and I are already at the hotel. You guys coming or what? The sun is almost up, for crying out loud."

"We're on our way, love," laughed Ella. "Did you get anything to eat?"

"I ran down a wild pizza and, well, you know, there's no crust left to tell the tale of its untimely demise."

"Wonderful. We'll be right there. Better book us a room, Kylie. It looks like a sunny day."

"We'll stay in my old room today, love. I'll book two extra rooms for Gudrun and Robert."

"Might as well just make it one, sweetheart. Robert will probably stay in Sally's room."

"Ella!"

"Sally? Woman, you've got some explaining to do," laughed Kylie. "See you soon folks."

Suddenly Sally stepped right into Robert's personal space and glared into his eyes. "Just what the hell are you doing to me, mister?"

"Absolutely nothing," he smiled delightedly. "You told me to behave myself, and so I am. Does this mean you're attracted to me, Sally?"

"If you don't stop teasing me, I'll..."

"Sally," he said softly as he took her shoulders in his huge hands, "I swear I'll never use the compulsion against you, if you swear to hold sacred the secret of my uniqueness. Is it a deal?"

"Deal, no tricks now..."

"No tricks, I swear it. May I use charm?"

Sally gazed into those ageless blue eyes and released herself to the madness her life had become. It had been years since she had been on a date, and here was a hunk like no other, the man of her dreams, giving her the attention she so desperately craved. "Alright big fella, but if you break my heart I'll put a wooden stake through yours."

"Noted, but you must know that wouldn't actually kill me."

"I know, but Ella says it hurts like hell." Everyone was still chuckling as the van got under way.

Hotel Musings

A s they reached the hotel, Gudrun had already retired to her room. The others swiftly did the same, and Sally found herself standing at her door with Robert beside her. "Do not be so frightened, Sally, I will not harm you." She did not respond, she just opened the door and let him inside.

"I've always disliked the smell of hotel rooms," he mused, "but this one is rather pleasant. You've inhabited this room for some time, Sally. Your scent is everywhere, making it all quite delightful. Sally, you're trembling, you're frightened. Please don't fear me so. I swear I will never..."

"That's not it," she breathed as she dropped her chin and looked away.

"Sally?"

"It, it, it's been a long time since..."

"Sally, come to me," he cooed softly.

"Why, Robert? Why me?'

Startled, he pulled back a bit to better see her eyes. They were filled with tears, and she was still trembling. "I don't understand the question, my pet. Please elaborate."

"I'm over thirty, overweight, as plain as a fence post, and have never... I mean, of all the women on this planet you could have, why me? I know you're sincere, Robert. You couldn't fool me that way. I just don't understand, why me?"

"Very well, my darling," he smiled as he gently pulled her closer once again. "You see, Sally my sweet," he whispered into her hair, "I'm an older gentleman, much older than you, so this will be a May/December relationship. Besides, you've been my constant companion for many years.

"Plain, my precious? Beauty is in the eye of the beholder, and I find your curves and long flowing hair to be quite beautiful. Best of all, darling girl, is the way you're always near. I felt you reaching for me as we disembarked the plane, and again while I hunted. This is a gift I've not experienced before, and it thrills me. Mine can be a lonely existence at times.

"You have never? Oh my darling girl, you certainly have in my dreams."

"Stop it," she blushed as she slapped at his arm and then smiled in spite of herself. "They were delightful dreams, weren't they?"

"They certainly were for me, Sally."

"And for me, Robert, but..."

"Now for the last part, I'm quite willing to wager that I've been celibate far longer than you have, my darling. My last wife passed away peacefully in eighteen eighty-three, and until I met you, I didn't believe I'd ever find another."

"But you've been married before," she breathed into his shoulder.

"Yes I have."

"More than once?"

"Several times."

"And you will be again."

"Was that a 'yes'?"

"Stop teasing," she giggled as she slapped his huge arm again, still keeping her face buried against his shoulder, "you know what I mean."

"The answer is yes, Sally. Forgive me, but I cannot change what I am. If you will consent to spend your days with me, I swear there will be no other during that time, or for a long time thereafter. No more than this can I give you, Sally. No more than this do I have to offer. Can that not be enough, or is this whole conversation a stalling tactic?"

"What??? Listen mister..."

"Yes dear?"

"I'm seriously starting to like the way you tease me out of my fears. I'm a very cautious person. Please be gentle with me, Robert..."

He stopped her ramblings with a kiss. It was very gentle, but lit a fire in her, one that had lain dormant for a very long time, and had only been allowed to burn in the dreams she had shared with Robert. Her Viking was real and here, in the flesh. She raised her hands and buried them in the hair brushing the back of his neck.

Robert felt her tongue tentatively touch his lips as her fingers clasped his head. He groaned into her mouth and deepened the kiss. Shaking slightly, he reached down, gathered her into his arms and carried her to the bed.

KYLIE LAY QUIETLY IN her lover's arms, her passion spent, and her head pillowed on Ella's breast. "Penny my love," whispered Ella.

"Huh?"

"A penny for your thoughts."

"Sorry lover, I was just worried about Sally."

"Worried?"

"Well, I mean, it's just that Sal isn't..."

"You mean she's not what most men consider desirable?"

"No...yeah. Please don't misunderstand. It's just that Robert is a hunk by any standards..."

"He's always been that way."

"Did you guys ever...?"

"Long, long ago and so very far away, my love. Remember what I told you about us. Once he learned to hunt on his own, I suddenly found him smug and insufferable. He accused me of being controlling. We quarreled and then parted ways. It's the way of things, my sweet.

"In truth, Robert is a very sweet and gentle man. He was, and still is, a fierce warrior, with a very strict code by which he lives, but he'll be very gentle with Sally. If she accepts him she'll be protected and pampered for the rest of her days, and he'll mourn for a century when she passes. Do not fear so, my beloved, Sally's in no danger from Robert. You know quite well Sally would run for the hills if she sensed any threat from him, and he could never hide that from her."

"Okay, I guess you know what you're talking about. So, you immortals are sensual creatures are you?"

"Oh my precious, you already know the answer to that one."

"All of you?" giggled Kylie.

"It's the nature of the beast," chuckled Ella as she affectionately nuzzled Kylie's hair.

"Indeed. Well then, alas for poor Gudrun, all alone in her room."

"If she chooses to be, yes, but don't worry about Gudrun. Did you not notice the effect she has on all men?"

"Oh yeah, she's a testosterone magnet all right. So, what do you think? Is she...?"

"I think you're trying to keep both my mind, and yours, from what's truly bothering you. Now stop this idle gossiping and tell me what is on your mind."

"Busted," sighed Kylie as she squirmed up in the bed to be eye to eye with her lover. "This will seem like a very long time to me, Ella, but it'll be only a heartbeat for you. You'll turn around and I'll be old, fat, and forgetting my own name..." Ella stopped her with a kiss.

"Yes my love," breathed Ella as their lips parted, "our time together will be quite short by my standards which is why I want to savor each and every moment. I will never take you for granted, not ever."

"You won't get tired of me, even when I get old?"

"No, I won't."

"Ella, promise me something."

"Of course, Kylie dear heart, whatever you desire. What do you need from me?"

"I want you to promise that, if I ever start to get forgetful, you know if I start to forget who you are or..."

"Kylie?"

"My grandmother had Alzheimer's, and when we went to see her, she didn't even know who we were..." tears were running down her cheeks now. "Ella, if I start to get like that, promise you will drink me completely dry."

"What???"

"To forget you would be the cruelest fate of all for me, Ella. If you drink my blood completely, I'll die still knowing you, and that you love me. That way I'll always be with you. Promise me now, please."

"The loss of mental faculties would be a cruel fate indeed, Kylie. Very well, if this is what you truly desire, I promise. Besides, if your memory does slip, you won't remember that I promised anyway."

"What??? Okay, that's it for you, Immortal!" declared Kylie as she seized a pillow and began to beat Ella with it. Ella shrieked with laughter and tried to hide under the covers, but Kylie pounced on her and kissed her deeply. "I mean it, Ella, promise me."

"Yes, my beloved, I promise you will always be with me. Go to sleep now, my darling, and know that you will not ever forget me. I won't let you."

THE SUN FADED BEHIND the tall buildings, and Sally lay awake against his shoulder, watching the world turn from natural light to artificial. Robert lay still, breathing deeply, yet he was acutely aware of his surroundings and the warm scent of the woman in his arms. "You can stop pretending," she giggled, "I know you're awake."

"How could you tell?" he asked softly, a smile on his face.

"I'm psychic, remember?"

"Of course, how silly of me."

"I felt you awaken, Robert. What have you done to me? I've never been this attuned to anyone before."

"If you can't recall what I've done to you, my girl, then I seriously think I must have lost my touch somewhere in the last century."

"Oh my love, your touch is just fine. Robert, what's going to become of me? Of us? I know your energy; I've always known you and this feels so right, like I always knew it would be somehow."

"Cast aside your fears, my beloved," he whispered into her hair. "As soon as Mobutu has been laid to rest, you and I shall marry, that is if you are so inclined."

"I am very much inclined, as you are well aware. Robert..."

"Sally, my darling, I am a well-respected antiques dealer in London. I'd love to marry you and carry off to Britain. If you prefer to remain in the land of your birth, I shall adopt a new identity and come here to be with you."

"Robert, can Ella truly defeat that evil creature?"

"Easily, my love," he replied with a smile. "You may have witnessed the charge of the great cat, but I've seen Ella in a full scale battle with not one, but two other vampires. They're both long dead and will not ever return. The key here will be to find him. That is one slippery son of... Sorry, forgive the language."

"Forgiven. So, should we arise and seek out the rest of our troops?"

"I'd much rather stay here with you for a year or two."

"As would I, Robert, as would I."

"But duty calls, and we must obey or Mother will be angry."

"And we don't want to make her angry," Sally smiled at him.

"No indeed, that we do not want to do." He kissed her cheek lightly then arose, stretched, and headed for the bathroom.

Sally joined him in the shower. "Robert, can I ask you something?"

"Yes love?"

"If you guys are, well, cats of a sort..."

"Why am I enjoying the shower so much? It must be the human part of me, for I do indeed enjoy the water. Come here to me now, and I'll wash your hair for you."

Much later they joined the rest of their friends in the dining room of the hotel. The humans were enjoying a good meal while the immortals just picked at the food. "You should try some of this, Miss Gudrun," grinned Agent Sawchuk as he offered her a taste of his steak.

She took the morsel and chewed it thoughtfully before swallowing. "Actually, I prefer mine quite rare," she grinned wickedly.

Suddenly Sally sat up, a look of fearful confusion on her face. "He's killed again," she breathed.

On the Hunt Again

They swiftly paid for the meal then headed for the mobile lab. Silence reigned as the truck sped through the streets towards the scene of the crime. It was a bit cramped in the van, and the closeness was beginning to show on the immortals. "Kylie, from now on, remind me to bring the car," sighed Ella.

"Sorry love."

"Ella, perhaps this might be a good time to begin the therapy," grinned Clyde as he tried to lighten the mood. With three vampires jammed this tightly together the humans wouldn't stand a chance if one of them cracked.

"Therapy, you're going into therapy, Mother?" Gudrun asked with an arched eyebrow.

"We all are."

"Excuse me?"

"Did you all not ask me to lead you?"

"We did."

"Well kiddies, if we're to be thrust into close quarters from time to time, we need the tools to help us cope. Clyde and Amanda are the best, and so I've asked them to help us."

"Capital idea," laughed Robert. "I see you're thinking three steps ahead as usual. All right, let us begin. Sir Clyde, Lady Amanda, what's our first move?"

"Focus on a common bond or goal," replied Clyde.

"Perhaps begin planning the demise of our serial killer," suggested Amanda.

Ella rose to her feet, balancing easily in spite of the rolling and pitching movements of the truck as it sped through the streets following its police escort. "Very well. It's unlikely that Mobutu will still be at the scene of the crime. If he is we kill him. If he's not, we must find him. Kylie, give us your thoughts on this."

"I think he'll be long gone by now. A normal human would return to the embassy where he's protected from the long arm of the law."

"So his lair is in an embassy," grinned Gudrun. "Very well then, we shall have to dig him out."

"Hold the phone here, Goldie," exclaimed Agent Sawchuk, "The embassy is off limits no matter what he does, unless his government will let us in. I've already tried that path and they won't allow us entry."

"I go where I please, Terry," Gudrun replied tartly, "whenever I choose to go there. I'm not bound by your rules any more than Mobutu is."

"Terry?" grinned Ella. "Why Agent Sawchuk, until this moment I was unaware that you actually had a first name."

"Yeah, well, I try not to use it."

"Why ever not?"

"Terry Sawchuk? That means nothing to you at all?"

"No, may I assume he is a man of note?"

"Terry Sawchuk was a hockey player in the old days." Agent Sawchuk sighed and his shoulders slumped. "Both my dad and grandpa were big fans, so..."

"And this is bad because...?"

"He played in the days before goal tenders wore masks. The man had no front teeth because he'd stick his face in front of a frozen puck traveling hundreds of miles per hour, if that was the only way to stop it. He never had the good sense to duck."

"And you don't want to be associated with such lack of good survival instincts. Very well then, you shall remain Agent Sawchuk."

"Not to me," grinned Gudrun, "you'll always be Terry to me."

"Alright, what's it going to cost me?"

"I don't want to hear Goldie from your lips ever again. Do we have a deal?"

"Deal, but why even bother? You could just make me stop."

"It's more fun to watch you bleed."

"Could you re-phrase that please," gulped Tommy, "you know, just for those of us who are faint of heart."

"It's more fun to watch him sweat?" Gudrun asked sweetly as she favored Tommy with a smile that made his knees shake.

"Much better," he replied as he blushed and looked away.

"Can we get back to the problem at hand now?"

"Of course, Agent Sawchuk," smiled Gudrun. "I see it this way, people, Kylie's right. He'll most likely retreat to his lair, and we must dig him out. Mother has the strength to kill him quickly, and I have the skills to penetrate the embassy. Ella and I go in after him, and Robert remains here."

"You had better have a good bit of reasoning to back up that last statement," said Robert, in a soft dangerous voice.

Gudrun met his eyes squarely. "Someone needs to protect our human allies."

"She's right, Robert," said Ella as she stepped between them. "Besides me, you have the best chance against him. Only you have a chance of defeating him should he double back to attack our allies and you know him well enough to know that's the sort of thing he might do. He'd torture and kill them all just to taunt us. I want you and Gudrun to remain here and guard these people."

"Forgive me, Mother," Gudrun said softly, "but you'll need me to get into the embassy. While you slept I've been developing these skills.

This is what I do, and I'm damn good at it. Robert must stay and I must go with you, there's no other way."

"There is another way," said Kylie.

"Kylie?"

"Agent Sawchuk has the combat training, and there isn't an embassy in this city that I can't get into if I want to. Agent Sawchuk and I can go with you, and so can Gudrun and Robert. Tommy can keep everybody else here in the van, and he can keep driving around the city until the deed is done. If the truck is on the move, Mobutu can't find it to attack."

"No way, Kylie..." began Agent Sawchuk, but she cut him off.

"Terry," she said as she went nose to nose with him, "you know damned well what we're up against here, and you know what has to happen. This is way outside the realm of sanity and you know it. Throw away the damned rule book on this one. Help us stop this thing."

He nodded his acquiescence, but Ella put in a veto. "No Kylie, I forbid it. Mobutu is far too dangerous for you to get involved. Stay here and let Robert..."

"Ella..."

"No Kylie, I forbid this. I won't allow you to put yourself in such danger. If I must I'll..."

"You'll what?" demanded Kylie as she got right in Ella's face. "You'll make me, and I won't know a damned thing for a week, and then it will be too late? Forget it, sister. I swear, if you put that damned spell on me, we're finished. If you do this it'll destroy the trust between us, and I will hunt you down and..."

Ella stopped her protest with a kiss. Kylie moaned softly as she melted into Ella's arms, and all her resistance was gone. "Have I told you yet that you're beautiful when you're angry?" purred Ella as their lips parted.

"Well, that's hardly fair," complained Gudrun.

"What?" asked Kylie as she turned to face the smiling blonde.

"When I got in her face like that, I awakened in Siberia with a note pinned to my chest, you get a kiss. You're spoiled rotten, but Mother's right. Facing down Mobutu is no place for you, Kylie. Personally, I don't plan to face him either. My job is to get Ella inside and then she does the nasty. You should stay here with Robert."

"Do I have nothing to say about this?" asked Robert.

"Hear me well, Robert," said Ella as she turned to face him squarely, "Kylie is precious to me. So are the others. If I must leave them, I'd prefer that it be in the care of Harald Fairhair, King of Nord Saxlund. You and you alone, would I trust with this; you and you alone, of all the others, have the strength and skill to defeat Mobutu in battle. Besides, there's the matter of Sally's safety to consider..."

"All right, I get the point," he sighed as his huge shoulders slumped. "However, I'm no jailer. I will hold no one here against their will. Will you trust me to keep you safe, good people?"

"You're the boss," said Tommy.

"Works for me," agreed the others.

"You truly were a king," breathed Sally.

"Once, my beloved, but that was so very long ago."

She sighed as she leaned against his arm. "It works for me, Robert. Stay with us, Kylie. Don't be so damned independent. Let Ella protect you. Let Robert keep you safe."

Just at this point the truck came to a halt, and the driver came around to open the door. Outside there was a scene of carnage surrounded with yellow police tape. Clara took her kit and, with Tommy in tow, set about checking out the crime scene.

Sally sat back and closed her eyes for a moment. "He's no longer here," she sighed at length.

"Very good, now we get to work," declared Ella. "Robert, take charge here, Gudrun, come. We must commandeer a ride back to my car."

"I'm coming with you," declared Kylie. Ella spun like a cat to face her but Kylie didn't back down from that penetrating gaze. "You'll need a getaway driver."

"You drop us off then you go far away," said Ella, her voice low and dangerous. "You keep moving until I call on the cell when we're finished."

Kylie nodded her head. She might be stubborn and independent, but she knew when to quit. She'd already pushed Ella too far, and she knew it. She fell into step with them as they approached a parked car near the police tape, a young man gawking at the spectacle. Kylie flashed her badge at the young driver and asked for a ride. He started to decline politely but Ella interrupted.

"*Do as she bids you,*" she commanded him, and, shaking fearfully, he got into his car. They followed and he swiftly returned them to the hotel. As soon as they arrived Ella commanded him to go home and forget he'd ever seen them. Gudrun ran up to her room then soon returned with a small bag.

They took Ella's car and headed to the embassy. By the time they arrived both Ella and Gudrun were wearing tight fitting spandex body suits and dark shoes. "You certainly came prepared," said Ella as she applied grease paint to her face.

"You taught me that yourself," grinned the blonde as she leaped easily from the car. "Come on." She vanished into the shadows.

Ella kissed Kylie lightly on the cheek. "Please forgive me for this, Kylie, but Mobutu is far too dangerous for me to risk you. Go now, and I'll call. Keep moving. Never stop in one place for more than a moment."

"Good hunting," Kylie said softly as Ella leaped after Gudrun. She sped away as her lover disappeared into the shadows.

AS THE GIRLS SPED AWAY, Robert turned to the others. "Alright my friends, we must prepare. What can we do to maximize the defensive capabilities of this van?"

"Are you serious?" asked Amanda.

"I'm quite serious. I'm more than willing to face Mobutu, if it comes to that, but not in such tight quarters. I'd like to tighten up this van then get outside. I'll remain near; Sally can reassure you of my presence."

"Who is stronger, you or him?" asked Agent Sawchuk.

"He is, but only just. The last time we struggled, he managed to overpower me. I intend that it shall not happen again. Have you weapons here?"

"There's my gun, plus a few more that belonged to Leon and Mendez. Right now, I'm the only one trained on them."

"Blades?"

"Ella said you might want these." Agent Sawchuk pulled a long bag from under the bench. "She left them here earlier."

Robert unzipped the bag and grinned his delight. He pulled out a long bronze dagger and a bronze short sword, both were razor sharp. "Well I'll be, her own blades," he mused. "She was wearing these when we first met. Perfect." With an ease born of long years of practice he slid the blades through his belt and pulled his coat over them.

"Robert?"

"I know, love, I know. The blades are unnecessary anymore, nor have they been for hundreds of years, but the tools of one's youth are always a comfort. That's why I still practice with blades daily. I find it comforting. Ella knows this of course. She also knows that if I'd had a good blade the last time I faced Mobutu, the outcome would have been much different."

"If he beat you, how did you survive?"

"He hadn't the strength to finish me. He thought he had, but obviously he hadn't. If he comes tonight, there will be a different outcome."

MOBUTU'S SCENT WAS strong in the air as they slunk along the wall. Gudrun ignored the gate, and all other obvious avenues of entry that were guarded by security cameras and alarms. With a leap that defied gravity she gained the roof, Ella right on her heels. Like a cat she crept along the eaves, peering over the side, until she found what she was looking for, a room full of armed men watching video monitors.

Softly she whispered in Ella's ear then turned back to the eave. Gudrun swung easily over the edge, and, clinging to the windowsill, peered through the glass. The men weren't paying attention, so she scratched at the sash. It took a few tries, but finally a man came and opened the window. Poking his head through the opening he looked about, expecting to find a cat or squirrel, instead he found a vampire.

Gudrun hung by one arm and grabbed his throat in the other hand, cutting off his voice and raising his head against the window, forcing it all the way open. With the window fully open she thrust him back inside and swung herself in behind him, Ella close behind her. Before the rest of the men could react, they were dead or unconscious, and the alarms disabled.

Like a hunting panther, Gudrun first peered into the hallway then slunk along it, testing the air with her nostrils. She had transformed into the half human / half tiger.

Together they searched every room one by one, but no Mobutu. At last they found his lair, in a hidden room deep in the basement. It was good that none of the humans were with them, as what they found would have sickened them. Several nearly dead and badly maimed humans hung from the walls in chains. The bodies of still others lay scattered about. There were several different altars to unknown gods and several ornate boxes upon the altars.

Ella was cursing softly as she dispatched the mangled humans. Their suffering was over at last. She set fire to some of the altar curtains then turned to go when an errand scent gently touched her nostrils. "Helga, I mean Gudrun, do you smell that?"

"It's Gina. That bastard has kept something of hers as a souvenir."

"You don't think he kept..."

"Where is it, we're nearly out of time!"

"Got it," exulted Ella as she swept up a rather ornately carved box from a gore bespattered altar. She cracked it open to find a freshly cleaned skull inside. "It's just as I thought. Let's go, he isn't here. We must return to the others as quickly as possible, for he's aware of them as well."

They quickly fled the embassy, leaving it in flames. As they reached the street Ella called for Kylie, and saw the headlights flick on a block away. "Blast that girl, she'll be the death of me," muttered Ella as she wiped the paint from her face.

"She's really gotten under your skin, hasn't she? Is that Gina's head in that box?"

"It is. Do you know the location of the bones?"

"I laid her in the crypt myself. I'll return that to her, with your permission."

"Then I place it in your care," replied Ella as she passed over the box and climbed into the car. "Kylie, I told you to..."

"Later, Ella, Mobutu is at the van," declared Kylie as she gunned the engine and ran a red light.

Battle Joined

While Ella and company sped through the streets, a maddened creature huddled in an alleyway. With the patience of the insane, he waited until he was sure they had found his calling card. Slowly he began to return, sniffing at the air constantly. She'd surprised him once. She wouldn't have it so easy this time.

"Ah, there it is," he muttered as the mobile unit that her human allies traveled in came into view.

Silently he watched and waited. There was no sign of that she-devil, but he could hear her humans within the vehicle. Listening carefully he learned that she'd gone to his lair to seek him out. With a chuckle of pure delight he moved closer. He'd torture and kill the human allies of the enemy, leaving them for her to find. The anticipation of the kill overrode his senses until it was too late.

WITH ROBERT'S GUIDANCE they had made the truck almost impenetrable. It had taken a bit of time, but the inside had been rearranged as well. Now anyone trying to enter without an invitation would be faced with several obstacles that were meant to slow him down. It wouldn't stop a vampire, but it would give them time to put a few bullets into him. It would give them a fighting chance.

Robert had caught an errant scent and sensed that Mobutu was near. He was lying atop the van, already changed into the half beast;

his coat with belt and blades lying at his side. He steeled himself and fingered the sword hilt affectionately. Slowing his heart rate, Robert settled down to wait. His patience was rewarded.

Ella and Gudrun had been gone for some time when Robert caught Mobutu's scent once again. This time it was stronger. Listening with all his senses, he heard a soft footfall. He also felt Sally's sudden fear. The centuries vanished as the warrior king tensed to spring.

Inside, Tommy had the surveillance equipment running. They saw as a shadowy figure crept from the alley and approached the van. They all held their breath as the latch was tested. Suddenly the door was torn away, and the nightmare was grinning up at them. He had no time to gloat, as a familiar voice sounded behind him, causing him to leap away.

"Hallo, Mobutu. Come meet your doom."

"Harald Saxon," hissed the misshapen creature as it leaped away, wildly licking at its fangs. "Didn't I kill you already?"

"Hardly." Robert had no time to say more as the thing attacked with a maddened vengeance. Robert was thrown against a building with enough force to shatter several concrete blocks. The thing hurled itself on him, but Robert wasn't there. Twisting to one side Robert lashed out with a huge fist and connected with the creature's skull. Mobutu went down under the force of that blow.

It was far from over though. Mobutu rolled aside just in time to keep from having his head crushed by a big boot. He spun on his back and lashed out with a foot catching Robert on the side of the knee. Robert went down and Mobutu leaped on him. Inside the van, Sally screamed.

Fangs sought Robert's throat and strong hands dug deeply into his neck trying to choke off his air. It could easily have been the end, but Robert had been a warrior long before he became a vampire. A hard elbow smash to the head knocked Mobutu off him, and then he was on top.

They struggled back and forth for some time, and it almost seemed as though the buildings were taking more damage, but both vampires were bleeding profusely. Suddenly Mobutu landed a telling blow and then sank his fangs deep into Robert's neck. A desperate twist and Robert was free, although bleeding badly. He rolled away across his coat which he had dropped close by for battle.

Mobutu leaped at him to finish him off, and then screeched as he tried to turn aside. Robert had come to his feet with that deadly short sword flashing. Mobutu was cut deeply in several places before he could retreat to a safe distance. Robert shrugged his huge shoulders then spun the blade expertly in the air before him as he advanced on his enemy. Mobutu turned and fled into the shadows. Robert didn't pursue him.

Robert stood like a monument to the god of war, blood flowing freely down the front of his shirt. He didn't react when Mobutu's mocking voice called out from the shadows. "Come to me, Harald Saxon. Come play in the shadows."

When Robert didn't respond Mobutu returned, slowly, carefully circling his prey. Robert moved to face him, but his movements were slow and awkward. Suddenly Mobutu feinted to the left then charged in on the right. He shrieked in frustration and fear as that blade magically leaped through the air and sought his throat. Again he retreated to the shadows, a terrible gash in his neck.

"Mobutu," called Robert, "come back to me. Come meet the fate you so richly deserve."

"You must come to me, Saxon."

"No, slime pig, I'll not play that game with you. I've beaten you, Mobutu, but I won't play your game. Besides, this isn't my hunting ground, and you're not my prey to kill. Ella will return soon, and the great cat will take up the hunt. My task is to prevent you from harming the humans within, and I'll do exactly that. Approach again and meet your fate."

Even as Robert spoke Mobutu charged from the side, slashing and swinging a club that turned out to be a human arm. The blades of a king lashed out again and the maddened killer fell, scrambling to escape. He was deeply wounded this time. Only by good luck was his life saved. Two cars came flying around the corner, their blinding headlights distracting Robert, and saving Mobutu's life.

As the lights temporarily blinded him Robert lashed out with his spinning blades. However, Mobutu didn't try to attack but, instead, fled for his life. One of the two racers screeched to a halt and the driver leaped out to run to Robert.

"Hey Jack, are you alright? "Oh shit..." he stammered as he got a good look at who was facing him. He tried to back away but wasn't able to escape in time. Robert's huge paw seized him, and he screamed as long fangs bit deeply into his neck. He struggled wildly at first, but then the fight went out of him, and he went limp in Robert's grasp.

With a snarl Robert thrust him away, and the young man sank slowly to the ground, weakly holding his neck where the vampire had bitten him. Terrified, he tried to crawl away, but Robert grabbed him and hauled him to his feet. "*You will forget this experience completely. You will leave this place now and never return. Go!*" As though in a trance, the man staggered to his car and raced away.

With a deep sigh, Robert leaned against the side of the van and allowed his form to return to human. He had taken terrible wounds in the fight with Mobutu, but the young street racer's blood was helping him heal. "Robert? Are you alright, Robert?"

"Sally, get back inside, quickly..."

"It's alright, lover, he's gone now. You beat him, but you didn't kill him. He's seeking a victim to help heal his wounds."

"Then we'd better go after him and finish him off," declared Agent Sawchuk as he stepped down, a heavy shotgun in his hand.

"No, Agent Sawchuk. Go after him and you'll grant his wish. He'll drink you dry then heal himself. I was fortunate to get enough to heal myself somewhat, but I'm in no shape for another battle, especially on his turf. We stay here and await our reinforcements."

"I can defend these folks if you want to go after him alone," Agent Sawchuk said softly.

"Mobutu is badly wounded, sir, and at his most dangerous. Were I well rested and well fed I would surely pursue him, but not as I am now."

"You're staying because of me, aren't you?" Sally said as she reached for Robert.

"Yes, my love. I've sworn to protect you, and that's just what I'll do, besides, I don't abandon my allies and leave them vulnerable to attack. I'll remain here as will we all. Once Mother returns, things may well be different." Robert clasped Sally's hand firmly in his own. Now that he had found her, he would protect her with his life.

"I just spoke to Ella," called Amanda, as she poked her head out of the van. "They'll be here shortly."

"So be it then," sighed Robert, as he leaned gently against Sally's shoulder.

"Robert, if you need to feed..."

"No, my dear Sally," he breathed as he lightly kissed her hair, "you're my lover and my life. You're not prey, nor will you ever be. Once Ella and Gudrun arrive, I'll be free to hunt. Until then, I'm just fine. Now, everybody back in the van. I'll remain on guard."

"There's no need, my love, he's gone. He won't return tonight. I get the sense that he fears you now. This one has no stomach for a fair fight. With both you and Ella here, he'll probably flee the city."

"That would fit the profile alright," said Clyde. "If he runs true to form he'll flee and live to plot for another day."

Just at that moment Kylie rounded the corner and screeched to a halt. Ella and Gudrun leaped out of the car even before Kylie got it stopped. "Where?"

"That way," replied Robert, pointing to the alley into which Mobutu had disappeared. "He's wounded, but alive."

ELLA SLIPPED INTO THE narrow alleyway, her senses on full alert. The scent of blood was strong in her nostrils; Mobutu's blood. The alley was empty, but the scent was fresh, Robert had wounded him badly. Her feral eyes could see the trail on the ground where he'd dragged himself along, fleeing desperately for his life. "Pity Robert hadn't been able to finish him off," she mused as she followed his scent.

The trail ran along the alley and out onto the street. Somehow Mobutu had regained his feet, but his flight had still been painful. With a growl deep in her throat, she read where he'd tried to feed, but the victim had been able to break free, Robert truly had defeated the mad one.

She stalked along the street until she found another alley. The scent was strong here, and she entered cautiously. Her night vision easily cut through the gloom of the alley and found the mangled body of an old street woman. Mobutu had managed to feed himself, but only just. The trail led out the other end of the alley and then disappeared. Ah well, it had been worth a try. Ella hurried back to Kylie.

"YOU DEFEATED HIM?" Gudrun asked Robert as Ella leaped away. Kylie tried to follow, but Gudrun grabbed her arm and held her back.

"I did. Actually it was Mother's gift that turned the tide of battle."

"Mother's gift?"

"Her blades. I always fight better with a blade in my hand."

"Really," she replied with an arched eyebrow. "Well I prefer guns, big guns."

"I hear that," agreed Agent Sawchuk.

Ella soon returned; the frustration clear on her face. "He had a car nearby. He's escaped once again, but he's suffered a second defeat. Are you alright, Robert?"

"Yes, but I need to feed soon."

"Did you break my toys?"

"No, Mother, I was very careful with them. Actually, they did make all the difference. He's still too strong for me to defeat at hand to hand, but he's no match for me if I have a blade."

"I'm well pleased with you, Robert, and you as well, Gudrun. Mobutu has fled once again, so we're stymied for the moment. Gudrun, take Robert hunting and be certain to feed yourself. I'll remain here until you return, and then I'll hunt. Tomorrow Robert and I will take up the trail again. Gudrun will head to Italy to restore Gina."

"Restore Gina?" asked Robert, "How?"

"Mobutu kept her head as a trophy and Mother found it at the Embassy," explained Gudrun. "I've already sent word to my people. A plane will be waiting for me as soon as I've fed."

Kylie waved her car keys at Gudrun and tossed them her way. Gudrun wasted no time in collecting Robert and driving away.

"Sally and Clyde believe Mobutu will flee the city now," said Amanda. "I must agree with them. He called you out and barely escaped you. He attacked your friends, and Robert nearly made an end of him. This town is now too hot for him and he'll flee."

"Kylie," said Ella as she turned her hard gaze on her lover.

"Ella, I'm sorry, I..."

"Are you always going to be so hardheaded and independent?" Ella asked softly as she reached for Kylie.

"Probably," sighed Kylie as she came to her lover. "Are you always going to be so darned bossy?"

"Probably. As I have said before, I'm quite set in my ways. Agent Sawchuk, how badly was Robert hurt?"

"He took quite a beating alright, but Mobutu got the worst of it. Robert's tougher than he looks, and he's wicked with that sword."

"The sword is as natural to Robert as breathing. I had those exact blades when I first met him. It took him only moments to disarm me completely. I had to put the compulsion on him just to keep my head. It was he who taught me the proper way to use them. He and Mobutu are well matched for strength, but with a blade in his hand Robert is the better man by far."

"So, what do we do now?"

"Now, Agent Sawchuk, my friend, we wait for our allies to return then it's back to the hotel for a good day's rest. If he truly flees the city it'll be up to Kylie to track him down."

"He can run, but he can't hide, not from me."

Approaching Showdown

For several days Kylie was glued to the computer, but no sign of Mobutu. Robert was fully healed now, and with Ella, spent much of his time at night, prowling the streets, all to no avail. Mobutu was not to be found.

Finally, Kylie got on his trail. Mobutu'd left town but returned a few days later and gone to ground. "My best guess is he's holed up somewhere near the burned out embassy."

"Then we'll focus our efforts there." Ella was determined and as patient as the great cat. Sooner or later Mobutu would slip up, and then she would have him.

Alas, it was not to be so easy. She caught his scent from time to time, but it always vanished. Ella hated trying to follow a scent in the city. It was too easy to just take a cab to somewhere else and the trail would be lost. Thus it was tracking Mobutu.

Ella was getting frustrated, and she was letting it show. Everyone tried to stay out of her path, but they weren't always successful. Realizing she was terrifying her allies almost as badly as Mobutu, she relented and placed a call to Gudrun in Italy. She would need all her resources.

TWO MEN ON THE MEZZANINE of an old warehouse spoke in hushed tones as a madman ranted and raven on the concrete floor below. This one called himself a god, but he was a mad god at best and the devil incarnate at least.

"I don't like this, Louie. He's gone completely fucking nuts."

"Quiet! He'll hear you. The guy's got ears like a dog, he hears everything."

The man below paused in his rant. "Come down, both of you. I have a task for you to complete."

They hurried down the stairs and approached respectfully. "What's up, Boss?"

"Listen carefully. This is what I want you to do." He explained his plan, but they didn't seem to be overly enthused. "You will obey me. I'll create the diversion to draw the enemy away so you can strike. Do not fail me in this, or I'll be very displeased, and hungry." Both men blanched then hurried away.

IT WAS NEAR DAWN, AND the team was gathered outside the van, which was parked near the burned out embassy. Ella was on edge as was Robert. Something wasn't right, all their primitive instincts were screaming of danger. Suddenly there was a scream about a block away.

Mobutu shook his victim them dropped him. He fled as Ella charged with Robert close behind.

Mobutu had planned to allow them to keep him in sight for a time, but she was too damn fast. Already transformed into the giant cat, she was gaining at an alarming rate. Mobutu signaled for his ride and leaped into the bed of the speeding truck. It was almost not enough. She hadn't slowed down, and found a burst of speed from somewhere. Her claws raked the tailgate of the truck before it gained enough speed to escape her.

The tiger was roaring in frustration as Robert caught up. He skidded to a halt, and then slowly backed away, unsure if he dared to approach. Slowly she shimmered back into a woman. Ella was cursing in an ancient tongue as Robert handed her his coat. "Your clothing is all shredded, you'll need this."

Even as he spoke there was a squealing of tortured rubber and the team's van raced away, escorted by several cars. A hail of gunfire was aimed at Robert and Ella to keep them back.

"A ruse," Ella said softly, gripping his arm tight enough to break bone. "Harald, they've got Kylie."

"Yes, and Sally. Mobutu has the upper hand for the moment."

"If he harms..."

"He won't, Mother. He'll use them as bait to lure you into a trap."

"I'm..."

"Mother, please listen. We can't help them now. We're of another age and out of our element here."

"What do you suggest?"

"We need Gudrun. This is what she does, and she does it well. We must await her return."

Ella allowed her shoulders to slump, and she leaned against him. There were tears in her eyes. Robert put his arm around her shoulders protectively, his own eyes as hard as flint. Robert would not only hunt Mobutu, but every human who had helped him as well.

"Take me home, Harald, sorry, Robert."

"No, you're right; I've become soft and complacent. It's time I became Harald Eldredsson once again. I had that maggot, but he escaped me."

"He escaped me as well, Harald. That scum is as slippery as an eel. We must find a way to finish him before he can harm Kylie and the others. Are you certain Gudrun can..."

"Oh yes. This sort of thing is what she does, and she is damned good at it. She'll know what to do."

"Then we shall return to my lair and await her return."

When they reached the apartment, Harald called Gudrun and got a piece of good news, she was already on her way.

Captive

They sat huddled together, in the open area of the warehouse. Armed men surrounded them, watching carefully. This was not going so well.

"Boss, these are Federal badges. These people are Feds. Oh man, we're in so much shit now."

"Be silent, or I will silence you permanently."

"Look, I don't want no part of screwing with the Feds like this," said one man as he began to back away. He screamed as Mobutu shifted and leaped on him. The automatic weapon rattled to the floor as he screamed out his last breath.

Mobutu drank greedily from the broken body before casting it aside. "Get rid of that, and know the same fate awaits anyone who refuses to obey me. *Obey me!*" Two men grabbed the corpse and dragged it away. The rest stood trembling, as did the captives.

Fighting his fear all the way, Agent Sawchuk struggled to his feet and stepped between Mobutu and the others. "Look, I'm the agent in charge here. You can let the others go; I'm the one with value to you."

"Be silent, you stupid fool. You have no value to me at all. I only want that one," pointing at Kylie. "That one is precious to the old hag, and it's that one's screams that will bring her within reach of my fangs. The rest of you are irrelevant. You remain alive only as long as you do not displease me. Take them away."

They were herded into a small windowless room and the door was locked behind them. Agent Sawchuk and Clara set to work looking for anything that might give a possible way out. Tommy looked scared to death as did Amanda and Clyde.

Kylie held Sally in her arms and crooned softly. Sally was terrified, but Kylie seemed to be clam.

"Kylie, how can you be so calm? That thing wants to kill us horribly, I just know it."

"Hush now, Sally, all of you. He can hear us as easily as a dog. Keep your voices down. We're not dead yet, Sal. Let's work on this and see what we can do from here to let Ella know where we are."

"How do you plan to let her know, Kylie? They took all our phones and those homing signal thingies."

"That's your job, Sal. Robert can feel you when you focus on him, so focus on him. At least then they'll know we're still alive. Try to send any memories you have of the trip here."

"We were locked in the back of the van, Kylie. We couldn't see or hear anything."

"Just do what you can, sweetie. We need to try every angle. Just sit down here in the corner and focus."

"Tommy, how the hell did they get close enough to take us so easily?"

"I don't know, Agent Sawchuk. They must have had some very sophisticated equipment to block us that way. Our surveillance didn't show a single blip until they were on us."

"Well, thankfully the only death so far was one of their own."

"You can say that again, Amanda," mused Kylie as she inspected the door hinges carefully.

"Forget it," sighed Agent Sawchuk, "this place is pretty airtight. We can't even reach the air ducts; the ceiling is too high."

"Maybe we could boost Sally up to that vent."

"Forget that, Kylie. You're the athlete; let the guys boost you up."

"Sally honey, that noggin of yours is the only communications device we have left. You have to go. If I go he could kill the rest of you or worse. As long as he has me, he might ignore your absence or just send a minion after you."

"I don't think we can make it anyway, Kylie," sighed Agent Sawchuk. "If Leon was still here I could get on his shoulders then Sally could climb up, but as it is..."

"Okay, I get it. So, what do we do now?"

"Now we wait."

"For what?"

Agent Sawchuk replied, "For Blondie to get here."

"Gudrun? You think..."

"It's what she does, Kylie. If I was Ella, that's who I'd send in."

HARALD WAS ON HIS CELL even as they took the elevator to Ella's apartment. "Peter, can you reach Gudrun?"

"She is already on her way to you with Gina, Robert. What's happened?"

"Mobutu has allied himself with human criminals. They've captured our allies including mine and Ella's chosen mates."

"This could be the beginning of the end for all of us. What must we do, Robert?" asked Peter.

"Bring them here, Harald, all of them," said Ella, as she stepped from the elevator and headed for her closet.

"I'm now changing my name back to Harald Eldredsson, Peter. Bring all the others and come here at once. Please bring me new identity documents as well. It's time I became the Saxon again."

Ella returned dressed once again. She passed Harald his coat as she spoke. "Tell them to hurry, Harald."

"We hear and we're already on the way," rumbled Peter's deep basso voice.

"So now we wait, my king." Tears of frustrated rage filled Ella's eyes, but she fought them back and sank into a chair.

Herald sat on the sofa facing her. "It's been a long time since you called me that."

"Too long; it's high time I started again, all of us."

"Ella?"

"I am a solitary huntress, Harald. I've learned much in my long lifetime. One important thing I've learned is to know my own limitations. I've failed here."

"No, Ella."

"Yes I have, and for good reason. I'm too solitary, too accustomed to doing everything on my own. I've hunted Mobutu, but he has eluded or escaped me at every turn. He must be killed and the damage he has done repaired if possible."

"Agreed."

"I have failed, Harald. I know it's because I don't have the skills to defeat him. You do."

"Me?"

"You, Harald. I enlisted humans to help me, but so did Mobutu. He has outwitted me and captured my friends as well as my lover. He's beaten me."

"No, Ella..."

"Yes, my king, and as much as it galls me, I must admit it. This has now escalated from a challenge of single combat to open warfare. This is where you excel. As a Saxon king you had no equal. I'm no leader, Harald; that's painfully obvious to me now. When you first called you asked me to lead you all. That task now falls to you. I now proclaim you King of the Immortals."

"Ella, I..."

"Harald, when you called you had already managed to band the others into a functional group, and it was clear they looked to you for leadership. I will gladly remain a member of this group, and a loyal subject of the king, but I beg you, take control of this situation before it gets any worse."

"You're serious, aren't you?"

"Completely."

"Ella, if you're serious about making me king..."

"I understand, Harald. I swear you will have my obedience and my undying loyalty. Please accept this."

"Very well, I accept, but the others will have to choose for themselves."

"As you desire, my king, so shall it be. What's our next move?"

"We await the arrival of our kin, and then we charge Gudrun with the task of removing the obstacles and retrieving our people. You're our strongest fighter, therefore, you will be charged with Mobutu's demise. I'll be your second and ensure there are no other interferences. This time we will not fail."

They sat in silence for a while then Harald's cell phone rang. "We're in the air, Harald. We're on a private plane. There's a small airport about an hour out of the city, can you meet us there?"

"Of course. Gudrun, what are you up to?"

"I'm taking a page from Mother's book. I confided in my team, found three that I could trust then put the compulsion on the rest. My trusties are with me as well as the rest of our people."

"Excellent. I have something else for you all to mull over. Ella has placed me in charge here. She has declared me king of our people, but I leave it up to you if you can live with this or not. You have until you land to decide." He closed the connection and sighed as he allowed the hand holding the phone to drop into his lap. "Well, there it is; I hope they'll come."

"Have faith in yourself. They'll come."

The phone in his hand began to buzz. He thumbed it open and then grinned as he read the message. "Well, at least they didn't turn the plane around. They've sent the coordinates of their landing site. Have you a map?"

"I have something better," smiled Ella as she rose and went to the computer. "Kylie's been teaching me. Let me see now, Google maps. Here we are, now let's find those coordinates and print off a map."

IT HAD BEEN HOURS WITHOUT a sound from outside the door. Agent Sawchuk had tried the door a few times, but nothing moved it. Kylie had tried to pick the lock, but to no avail, the door must have been braced from the outside. Finally they heard a noise outside, a scraping as though something heavy was being moved. At length the door opened and a hard faced man cautiously looked in. "You, the man in charge, get your ass out here, and no tricks."

Agent Sawchuk walked out slowly, his hands spread wide. "Over there, get moving." A push from behind moved him in the right direction, the door of the prison slamming shut behind him. He was returned to the big open warehouse where Mobutu was waiting for him. He thought he was about to meet his end, but he got a surprise.

"Ah, it's the man in charge." Mobutu grinned at him as he stepped into the agent's personal space. "I have a task for you, Mr. 'I am the agent in charge.' I'm going to set you free. You will take that awkward vehicle of yours and return to that ancient hag. You will bring her here as the sun sets tomorrow. If she tries anything foolish, her paramour will be killed in a most horrible way. She must come with you alone. If there is any sign of treachery there will be a death she does not want. Go now."

Agent Sawchuk was half dragged half pushed to the van and climbed inside. The huge doors opened and he instantly knew where he was. Cursing softly, he drove out the gates and back into the city. As soon as he spotted a pay phone he stopped and, scooping a few of the quarters from the ashtray, leaped out to place his call. There was no answer at her apartment, so he tried her cell. She answered on the first ring.

"Ella, it's Agent Sawchuk."

"You escaped. How..."

"No, Ella, he set me free to bring you a message. I'm to bring you to him at sundown tomorrow. You're to come alone."

"Meet me at my apartment, Agent Sawchuk. I'll be there in about two hours."

"I'll be parked right outside, Ella." With that he was gone.

AS ELLA PUT AWAY HER phone the plane taxied to a stop right in front of them. Gudrun was the first on the ground, followed by a small woman with a Mediterranean appearance. "Gina, it is good to see you, I was afraid we had lost you."

"It is good to see you again, my King. Mother, I believe I have you to thank for my return. I've come to do what I can to repay the favor."

"Your presence is welcome, all of you. What's your decision as to our king?"

"We will serve King Harald," rumbled the deep voice of the short stocky man with flashing eyes. "If we're to survive in this new age, we'll need to use all our resources. You're the eldest and most powerful as well as the wisest. We thought you should lead us, but we can see the wisdom of your decision. Harald has the experience of leadership and command. Hail the king!"

"Hail the king." It was a full chorus, no dissenters.

"Thank you all. I swear I'll do all in my power to protect and lead you. Right now we have a situation on our hands. Gudrun, our allies have been taken by Mobutu with the aid of a criminal organization he has allied himself with. Agent Sawchuk was sent back with a message. Ella is to be taken to the place where he has the captives; she is to go alone. I'm far more accustomed to open warfare than this sort of thing. I want you to take charge here; we're all at your disposal."

"Yes, my lord. Eric!" One of the three men stepped forward. "We need transportation and small arms, lots of them. We have only a few hours to prepare, so be swift. Here is the address of where we will meet."

He nodded to Gudrun as he accepted the card with Ella's address on it. "Are we going in at sundown?"

"Don't we always?"

He chuckled then turned and motioned the other two to follow. They trotted away towards the large terminal building.

"Now then, people, we should find Terry and pick his brain so I can make a plan. I need to know the layout of that place and there isn't a lot of time to prepare. I'll need everyone's instant obedience on this, there can be no hesitation."

"You'll have it, Gudrun." Ella's eyes were hard and everyone gave full agreement. Just then a limo pulled up and Eric got out to hold open the door.

"What took you so long?" asked Gudrun as she got in the car. He just chuckled. Ella and Harald got back in her car and led the limo to her place. Agent Sawchuk was waiting for them.

"Miss Gudrun, damn, am I ever glad you're here," he said as they all crowded into the elevator to Ella's apartment.

"Why Terry, I think you missed me." She was grinning as they entered the living room.

His mouth worked for a moment then he sighed and shook his head, a grin playing at his lips. "Okay, yes I did, but we need to focus now. I assume you know what happened."

"I do, and I'm going to get them back."

"You do that; I'm going after that freak."

"Did you just use the f-word, Terry? I don't think I like that."

Any sane man would have run at that note in her voice, but Agent Sawchuk wasn't sane anymore. "Dammit, Blondie, that's not what I meant, and you know it." He was fairly trembling. "That bastard has terrorized this city, killed several of my friends, and now has more of them in his hands. I'm going to make him dead."

"Yes we are, Terry," she said, reaching out to grip his arm gently. "Keep it together now and help me here. Tomorrow at dark we take him down and Ella is going to make sure he never comes back."

"For the love of the gods, Gudrun, just put the compulsion on him so we can get the information he's carrying." That voice went silent as she turned her icy gaze on the offender.

"Terry is a friend, Jakob. Compel him and I'll personally rip out your throat. Now everybody get a grip. Eric will be here soon then we'll make our plans. Terry, sorry, Agent Sawchuk..."

"Call me Terry, Miss Gudrun. Agent Sawchuk got sloppy and now Terry has to go where no sane man should go."

"You could stay here, Agent Sawchuk." Ella gripped his arm gently. "This is beyond your human capabilities, no one would fault you."

"I would, Ella. Those people were my responsibility and I let them down. I don't care how damn strong and fast that monster is, give me a gun big enough and I'll bring him down."

"Ella will tear him apart fast enough, Terry. We just have to get her close enough. Ah, there's Eric." Once the three mercenaries were in the room, Gudrun continued. "All right, here are the assignments. Ella, you will be in the most danger as he will surely shoot you first. Eric will have a Kevlar vest for you. Terry, you deliver Ella, and then get the hell out of her way. Eric, you and I will lead; the rest of you will accompany us. Vasily, did you get a rocket launcher? Good. We're going in first. Terry. Give us everything you know, everything you saw, heard, or smelled about that place."

"Okay, he's got them in a warehouse inside the international customs compound. That's off limits, officially, but he took my badge, so I'm off the job. The street runs through a gate and down between a long row of buildings, warehouses. There's a dock at the end." He went on to describe the buildings, heights etc., and then he started on the target building. He spoke of exits, vents, inside layout, hiding places, and so on. They were all impressed with his attention to detail.

"That's good intel, Agent," said Eric. "I'm feeling better about this already. It should be a piece of cake."

"There's one problem, Eric."

"What's that, Agent?"

"The bastard can hear a pin drop a mile away and he can smell anything within a hundred yards."

"I've got the cure for that, right, Boss?"

"Right, Jimmy," grinned Gudrun. "Don't worry, Terry, we've done this before. Now, it's almost dawn. Everybody get some rest."

THE SUN WAS JUST DROPPING behind the buildings on the horizon when the van driven by Agent Sawchuk returned to the warehouse in the compound. He'd driven slowly once past the gates and watched in awe as the immortals raced across the rooftops. Even the three mercenaries were damned fast, managing to keep up with their leader. They silently swarmed the roof of the warehouse as he drove through the door, leaning on the horn.

Mobutu was incensed as they arrived. "Stop that noise, are you trying to burst my ear drums?"

"That's not such a bad idea at that," said a hard eyed Ella as she stepped down from the van. Mobutu's men swiftly searched the van then pronounced it empty.

With a signal from Mobutu's hand, Kylie was dragged to him, a gun at her head. He laughed cruelly as Ella fought to remain still.

"If you want this to live..." he got no further as there was an explosion outside. A noxious odor wafted through the open door. Ella nearly choked, but she fought it. Mobutu was cursing wildly, still holding Kylie by the hair, as he directed his men outside to investigate.

"If you want this one to live, you will do as I say." Mobutu was now holding a gun to Kylie's head. "Do you know what this is; you putrid stain on the earth? It's a gun, and it's the great equalizer. All your great strength will not avail you now."

"Stop raving like a madman and tell me what you want." Ella was cold now, prodding him.

"What I want is to kill you in battle," he slavered. One of his men tossed him an automatic weapon. He caught it with ease. "This little toy will even the odds, old woman. You have your cat, and I have my gun."

"Release Kylie and you shall have your wish, madman." Ella began to move slowly to her left as she spoke. Mobutu eyed her warily.

"Perhaps I will kill her first..." The words were barely past his lips when a shot rang out. The weapon leaped from his hands. Mobutu spun with alarming speed then froze in shock. Kylie crawled away to hide behind a thick post where Gudrun was motioning her to come.

Mobutu trembled in mixed rage and fear as he saw his men lying face down on the floor, an immortal standing over each one. There were also three humans with heavy weapons trained on him. Even if he wanted to attack, Harald the Saxon was protecting them, a wicked looking blade in each hand. "All of you? Here? How???"

Mobutu got no further as the deafening roar of the big saber tooth sounded behind him. With a lightning move he spun about and dove for the fallen weapon. He came up shooting, but the cat was already on him, battering aside the weapon and knocking him back, great claw marks streaming blood down his chest. Blood trickled from the cat's ribs and another wound on her skull. The wounds only served to piss her off. She roared her challenge again.

Mobutu tried to escape, but the cat was too fast. She was on him instantly, battering him back into the open space in the giant room. Again and again he tried, but each time she drove him back. At last he turned at bay, determined to fight. With lightning speed he attack, but she was faster, stronger, and he was beaten down. Each time he struggled to his feet she beat him to the floor once again.

In desperation Mobutu feinted one way and leaped the other. He came up with the gun and opened fire as she leaped on him, knocking the gun away and seizing his neck in her powerful jaws. The cat flopped on her side, holding him from escape and raked at his struggling body with her back paws, her claws rending the flesh from his bones and the life from his body.

As he ceased struggling the cat leaped to her feet and roared her challenge again. A swipe from a huge paw and the head of Mobutu went rolling across the room. Still roaring, the cat ripped and shredded the body for several moments more. Kylie made a motion as though to go to her, but Gudrun restrained her. "Not yet, little sister; let her vent her rage and change back first."

Kylie nodded and looked at Ella again. The huge tiger was spattered from head to toe in blood, some her own and some Mobutu's. Her own wounds were sealing shut even as she paced and roared. Finally she stopped and stood still, and then shimmered in to Ella. Ella was still aroused and ready for battle, her eyes fiery and her freshly sealed wounds still new pink flesh. Kylie rushed into her arms.

"Ella, are you alright? Are you hurt? Do you need...?"

"Hush now, Kylie, I'm fine, and now that I have you safely in my arms I need nothing more."

"No? How about some clothes?" Gudrun was grinning as she passed Ella the backpack. With a nod of thanks and a wry smile Ella accepted the clothes and dressed herself.

"You were correct, my King," said Ella as the others approached. Agent Sawchuk had already brought the rest of the team out of their prison. "Gudrun was the perfect choice to lead this excursion. Gudrun, you were magnificent. I was aware of the snipers, but would have had little chance against them all. As you've said, you're very good at what you do."

"She's the best," grinned Eric, "and now I know why."

"Indeed she is," agreed Harald. "Gudrun, you and your men dispose of the body. Agent Sawchuk, can you get access to a crematorium?"

"I can."

"Then you dispose of this and bring me the ashes." Harald stabbed the head of the dead Mobutu with his blade and held it out to the agent. He took it and dropped it into a bag that Clara had produced from the back of the van. "Terry, do this, then take your people home. We won't put the compulsion on any of you; we'll trust you to keep silent about our existence."

"We'll do more than that, Sire or King, or..."

"Harald is fine, Terry."

"Harald. You and your people have just saved all our lives as well as the lives of millions of people. You'll need friends amongst us humans if you're going to survive long term. My team has a wealth of skills that can help you, and we want to."

"Accepted with gratitude, Agent Sawchuk. Ella, this city is your hunting ground, but it's large and there's room for us all here. I'd like to establish our headquarters here, if you don't object."

"I have no objection, my king. I believe that's wise. Perhaps my apartment can serve until better arrangements can be made."

"So be it."

"Robert, what's going on?" Sally's voice was soft and unsure. Watching Ella in battle had unnerved her somewhat.

"It seems I've become a king again, Sally, my love." Harald held her gently and lightly kissed her hair. "I am now King of the Immortals, and you are their Queen."

"Forgive me, my King, but this mission is not yet complete."

"Yes, Gudrun, you're right. Advise us."

"Terry, take your team, including the Queen and the Champion's Lady, and get out of here. Sire, take your people back to the new headquarters. My team will finish the job and report to you there. Quickly now, every moment wasted is a danger to us all."

"What about those men?" Sally was pointing to Mobutu's henchmen, who stood quietly under guard.

"I'll take care of that myself." Gudrun sighed as she saw Sally's face. "I'll put the compulsion on them, my Queen. They won't be harmed. Quickly now people, we've wasted too much time here already. Ella, perhaps as the Champion you should ride with the humans. If trouble develops they should have protection."

"A watchdog? Don't trust me, Blondie?"

"I trust you, Terry," sighed Gudrun. "This is champion's privilege; she won the battle; she gets the girl."

"Right, sorry, Miss Gudrun."

"You can make it up to me later, now get moving, all of you."

They did. The immortals seemed to vanish into the recesses of the warehouse. The humans, with Kylie tucked under Ella's arm, piled aboard the van and it slowly drove away.

An Unclear Future

As the van cleared the gates then sped off into the city, Sally turned to Ella with the questions they all wanted to ask. "Ella, can you tell us what's happened since we were captured?"

"Yes, Sally. Harald has changed his name back to the original Harald Eldredsson. He's been declared king of our people."

"How did that happen?" asked Kylie.

"I made it so, my darling. I hunted Mobutu and he escaped me time after time. He'd beaten me. When he took you, I knew he had beaten me. I demanded Harald become our king and take control; the others agreed with me. He placed Gudrun in charge of bringing us safely out; my task was to kill Mobutu. I'm pleased to say I've finally done so."

"So, if Robert, I mean Harald, is King, what does that mean for us?"

"As his mate, you will become Queen, Sally. We'll do our best to protect and obey you. We're all quite old, Sally, and, as surprising as it may seem to you, we're more comfortable in a monarchial society. Harald will make you his queen, then he'll call on all of you as well as all of his own people to advise him. He'll be a fine king, as he was once before."

"What does that mean for the rest of us?" asked Amanda.

"Harald will want to keep this team together; I'm certain of it. You're all invaluable to us. Should any of you wish to leave, a compulsion of forgetfulness will be placed upon you and you'll be set free."

"I'd rather stay," smiled Amanda. "I'm sure there'll be lots for me to do." The others all agreed, and the group seemed to relax at last. They'd been rescued and the monster had been slain.

At length the van stopped at a veterinary hospital. "Okay, Ella," called Agent Sawchuk, "let's get this done."

"You go ahead, Terry, I trust you."

"I know you and Blondie do, Ella, but the rest of your people don't know me. I want you to be able to report that the king's command has been carried out, and I want them to be comfortable with that. If you watch me get it done, they'll trust that."

"Very well then, let's be about it." She followed him to the building door where he rang for an attendant. A sleepy looking man appeared and asked with they wanted. Agent Sawchuk explained they had a dead cat in the bag and it needed to be cremated at once.

"I'll have to see it first," he muttered sleepily.

"Hear me, you have looked into the bag and seen a badly diseased cat's body. It must be cremated at once."

"That'll have to be cremated right now," shuddered the man as Ella stepped back from him. "Follow me." He led them into the crematorium and placed the bag into the receptacle. He then closed the doors and started the fires.

A short while later Ella returned to her apartment where Harald and the other immortals were gathered. Gudrun and her men had already returned.

"It's done, my king," said Ella as she placed the small box of ashes on a side table. "What's to be done with the ashes?"

"Gudrun has disposed of the remains in the sea," replied Harald as he pulled Sally close. "The ashes of the skull are to be taken to a remote place on the land and scattered into the winds."

"I'll do it myself," sighed Ella as she sank into a chair.

Kylie sat on the arm of the chair and put an arm around Ella's shoulders. "I'll go with you, sweetheart," smiled Kylie.

"Good, for I have an idea."

"What do you have in mind, Ella, my love?"

"Once we scatter the ashes, I'll change into the great cat; you will climb onto my back and hang on as I give you the ride of a lifetime. It's been several hundred years since I was able to race across the plains and I feel the need to stretch my legs."

"Oh baby, that sounds like fun," grinned Kylie.

"First you must hunt, and then heal, Ella," said Harald kindly. "Those bullets took a toll on you."

"As you command, Sire," smiled Ella as she rose, patted Kylie on the shoulder, and then stepped into the elevator.

Sally came and sat beside Kylie, and together they watched as her lover and soon-to-be husband, called his people around him and began to lay the plans for a new kingdom that would exist within her own society, a kingdom of which she would be Queen. With Mobutu dead and the threat of his killing madness removed, there promised to be busy and joyful days ahead.

Three days later, Kylie stood on a rocky knoll at the edge of the Great Plains and watched as Ella scattered the ashes of Mobutu's skull into the wind. That monster would never return!

With a delighted smile for Kylie, Ella cast aside the box that had contained the ashes. She dropped her coat, stepped out of her boots, and then, standing naked in the sun, beckoned Kylie closer.

As Kylie stepped towards her, Ella shimmered into the saber-toothed tiger. The great cat shook herself and gave a growling purr sound as she lowered her shoulders. Kylie climbed onto her back, grabbed on tightly to the cat's coat and clamped down hard with her legs. She squealed with glee as the great cat leaped away and raced across the open plain for the first time in centuries.

The end.

Author's note. A number of years ago I was challenged to write a vampire story. (They were quite popular at the time.) I agreed, but wanted to put a different spin on it. The tale of the tigress was the result. However, that led to several more. So... next for the werewolves.

Shapeshifter

by

Prudence MacLeod
Copyright, September 2015

Second edition.
(Formerly titled Children of the Wolf.)

Cornering a Killer

C ursing softly, and wishing for a fur coat as she trudged through
the snow in human form, the vampire shivered. Ah, to hell with
it, she stripped off her clothes and buried them in the snow before
changing her form into the sabre-toothed tiger; the cat could track the
maddened killer more easily, and she had a fur coat.

THE TALL WOMAN TRUDGED along behind the three men,
stepping in their tracks to make travel through the snow easier. The
cold wind was blocked somewhat by the trees, but she was aware of its
bite on her face. Immediately in front of her walked the burly form of
her boss and buddy, Agent Sawchuk. For the past number of years they
and their team had worked the tougher cases together, dealing with
that which no other agency could handle. Working for the vampire
king was much the same.

To the front of the small procession walked two of the local
deputies, a couple of good old boys. They carried their heavy hunting
rifles at the ready as they watched the trail before them. Suddenly
they stopped, confused. The taller of the two men spoke softly. "Agent
Sawchuk, look at this. Your tracker's footprints stop here. Her backpack
is there. It looks like she was taken by a big cat."

"A really big cat, Sam," said the other deputy. "I've never seen cat
tracks like that. These tracks are way too big to be a puma. Could a tiger

or lion gotten loose from that circus that passed through a few weeks ago?"

"Could be, Gordy," mused the first man as he checked his rifle and jacked a round into the chamber. He set the safety then began to study the tracks in greater detail. His companion did the same. "If it did, it's a hell of a big one by the size of those tracks."

"Sam, the woman's tracks just disappeared. That cat must have carried her off."

"Then why isn't there any blood, Gordy? No boy, this makes no sense at all. Agent Sawchuk, I hate to be the one to tell you this, but it looks like your tracker has been killed by some sort of giant cat. You and your partner better stay close behind us; that cat could be anywhere."

"The tracks suggest the cat is tracking our killer, Deputy. We should follow along."

"You don't seem too upset by the death of your tracker."

"She's not dead; she's with the tiger."

"What???"

"She's with the tiger, probably catching a ride, tracking the killer. She'll find him, and probably deal with him if he puts up a fight. I'll ask you to stand down your weapons."

"What? With a tiger on the loose? Stand down my weapon? There's no way in hell..." he got no further as he felt the cold metal of a gun by his ear. The woman was pointing her pistol right at his head.

"As the agent in charge, I command you to stand down your weapons," repeated Agent Sawchuk.

"As a woman with PMS and a gun at your head, I suggest you do as he says." The hard look in her eye left no room for argument. They lowered the rifles.

"Just what the hell is going on here, Agent?" Grudgingly, the deputy passed over his rifle as he spoke.

"I'll tell you," replied Agent Sawchuk, as he removed the magazine from the rifle, turned the weapon on its side and ejected the cartridge from the barrel. The round arced high into the air and he caught it deftly. A flick of the wrist popped it back into the magazine which he then clipped back into the rifle. Slipping the safety back on, he passed the rifle back to its owner. "We don't want you boys shooting anything you shouldn't. Now, keep the safeties on and don't shoot unless I tell you to."

"If either of you two even thinks about shooting my tiger, I'll blow your brains all over this mountain." Kylie spun her side arm back into its holster then retrieved the backpack.

"Your tiger?"

"My tiger. She and Ella are tracking the killer right now. They'll find him, probably kill him, and your town will be safe once again."

With a look of disbelief and fear, one of the deputies looked at the sky then spoke. "We should be heading back; there's a storm about to break and I don't want to get caught out here in a blizzard; especially not if there is a crazy woman with a tiger and a killer running loose. We can pick up the trail after the storm passes."

"Sorry boys, but we go on," sighed Agent Sawchuk.

"Then we'd better get a move on," growled the deputy as he slung his rifle over his shoulder and set out on the tracks of the tiger.

Kylie took up the rear again and continued to plod along. She was tired, too tired. They had been on the trail of this killer for weeks. She'd eventually tracked him to this small town, but then Ella had taken over as tracker. Deep woods stuff was definitely not Kylie's forte.

This hunt had started with the queen's nightmares. For several days she'd awakened, screaming, from dreams of gigantic wolves hunting and killing children. At the first sign of a murder the team had grabbed the case and set out. Kylie had no idea where the trail would end, but she hoped it would end soon. She was tired and cranky, and so was Ella. A cranky shape-shifting vampire is no fun to live with.

Kylie's reverie was broken by the battle roar of a sabre-toothed tiger. "Kylie, you take lead," barked Agent Sawchuk. as he stepped back to let her pass. "Remember boys, I'm right behind you. Don't shoot until I tell you to."

The tiger roared again, but its voice was mixed with barking growls of another animal. "So you let the woman go first?" sneered the deputy.

"It's her tiger," replied Agent Sawchuk, a grin playing at the corners of his mouth. "It'll kill anyone else who gets near unless Kylie's there. You follow her, and I'll follow you."

They caught up to Kylie a few moments later. She was standing at the edge of a clearing. In the small open space, a battle raged. The sabre-toothed tiger was there, but so was something else. It was a huge wolf, yet with almost manlike features. It was horribly fast and savage, but it was no match for the sabre-tooth.

The big cat had the wolf creature trapped against a cliff face. With nowhere to run, the beast turned at bay. As lithe and fast as the wolf-man was, the cat was equally as fast, and far stronger. The cat was a mountain of rippling muscle, especially in the front quarters. A swat from one great paw sent the creature crashing back against the rock face. It leaped back to its feet, searching madly for an avenue of escape.

There was none. There was only the curving face of stone soaring above, or the long fall to the frozen lake far below. The forest path was blocked by the tiger. In desperation it attacked the cat.

The battle was fast and furious. Both were bloodied when it was over, but the wolf man was down with the cat roaring above him. Knowing his end was near; the creature's features shifted slightly. He looked almost human, pleading as he reached toward the cat.

"Touranga engure astan oristle agnon." The words came with difficulty from those misshapen jaws, but the pleading in its eyes was easy to read. The big cat tilted her head sideways for a moment and the beast repeated the phrase. She backed away slowly and he staggered to his feet. With a nod of thanks to her he turned and leaped out into space, making no sound as he plummeted to the frozen lake far below. The ice shattered on impact and the broken body of the wolf-man sank into the icy waters. The body of a naked man would be found in the lake months later.

The tiger looked over the cliff for a moment then she turned back. The people at the edge of the clearing were all in shock, but the tall girl stepped forward. "Come to me, my darling girl," she spoke softly. Eyeing the others closely, the big cat came to the dark skinned woman, growling deep in her throat. Everyone stood very still as that mass of rippling fury slowly came to the woman and rubbed against her side.

"Here, my beloved beauty, here's Ella's backpack. Can you take it to her please?" Kylie rubbed the cat affectionately on the neck then the huge animal turned back to the forest, the backpack in its jaws. She stopped once to snarl at the two deputies then vanished into the trees.

"What the hell just happened here?" asked one of the deputies as they shook off the spell of fear cast by the presence of the tiger.

"We found the killer and he fell to his death," replied Agent Sawchuk.

"That the official version?" asked the second deputy.

"That's what will go in my report," replied the agent. "Do you want to write up how a sabre-toothed tiger fought a wolf-man and chased him off a cliff?"

"The official line sounds good to me, right, Gordy?"

"Oh yeah, we say anything else and we'll get locked up somewhere. What the hell was that thing anyway?"

"The military and secret government labs have been experimenting with genetic manipulation for years," sighed the special agent. "Things haven't always gone right, and sometimes things slip through their fingers."

"So, you guys are the clean-up crew?"

"Ah-huh, you could say that."

"But if we do, you'll have to shoot us," sighed the other deputy. "Okay, we've got it. Is that where you got the tiger, miss?"

Kylie smiled at the new note of respect in the man's voice. The colour of her skin didn't seem so important now. "Yes indeed," she grinned, "raised her from a cub. She'll find Ella, drop off the backpack then return to the van."

"So, where is your tracker?"

"I've been checking for signs of others like that lurking about." That rich contralto voice belonged to another tall woman. Both deputies straightened up a bit as Ella stepped into view. She was carrying an empty backpack. "He was alone. We need to hurry before the storm hits. There is nothing more for us to do here."

Both men had questions on their lips, but the three government agents set out, so the deputies followed close behind. It was a long hike back to the vehicles, but it was all downhill.

Somewhere along the way the deputies found themselves at the front of the line. The winds were picking up and the snow starting to fall by the time they reached the wrecked car of their fleeing killer. Their own vehicles were parked close by.

"Say, tracker, wasn't that backpack full when you joined us in the clearing up on the ridge?" The deputy was gazing quizzically at the pack Ella had just tossed into the back of the big four-wheel drive they had rented.

"No, whatever made you think that?" Ella climbed into the seat beside the pack with her back turned so he wouldn't see her smile.

"I could have sworn that dang thing was full," he muttered as he climbed into the truck with his partner.

"What was full?" asked Gordy as he gunned the engine and set out along the road.

"Her backpack."

"You think she stopped to dispose of something?"

"Yeah, and it was probably evidence."

"Who cares, Sam, the feds have the case, the evidence, and we're rid of a killer. It all works for me. All I want now is a hot meal and a cold beer."

"Ah, you're right, Gordy. There's no point wasting energy on it; they'll never really tell us anything anyway. Let's get home before this weather gets any worse."

Agent Sawchuk drove a bit slower than the two local men. The snow was falling faster and he was in an unfamiliar vehicle. As he focused on the road ahead, Kylie turned to Ella who was in the back seat. She reached for her lover's hand and squeezed it gently. "Ella, honey, are you all right?"

"Eh? Oh, yes, my darling Kylie, I am fine. I wasn't wounded all that badly and the damage has healed all ready."

"That's not what concerns me, sweetheart. You're being awfully quiet."

"Sorry, I'm just a bit disturbed by what happened up on that mountain."

"Ella, can you tell us what that thing was up there?" asked Agent Sawchuk, still tightly focused on the road ahead.

"I'm not certain, Terry, nor do I know what it said to me. I do know it was pleading with me for something, but it wasn't asking for mercy, at least not for itself. I only wish I could remember that phrase."

"Not to worry, my kitten, I have the whole show recorded on my phone."

"Kylie, you're a genius. Terry, we have to report to the king before you officially report in."

"I agree, but first I have to get us back to the hotel in one piece. This storm is really picking up." They continued on in silence for some time before the four-wheel drive forced its way into the hotel parking lot.

They fought their way through the storm and into the hotel lobby, shaking snow from their clothes and stomping their feet to clear their boots. They got a look of disapproval, yet nothing was said, as they picked up the room keys and headed for the elevators.

The girls were barely inside the room with the backpack on the spare bed when a light knock came at the door. Kylie opened it and let Agent Sawchuk in. He sank into a chair and passed a full wine bottle to Ella who eyed it suspiciously. "Wine, Terry? What's this for?"

"It's not wine, Ella, it's blood. I brought it along just in case of emergency. You've been in a battle and you haven't fed for days. This should tide you over until we get back to New York."

"Terry..."

"Ella, you can't go hunting in that," he sighed, gesturing at the storm outside.

"Agreed," she said, as she relaxed into her chair. "Where did you get this?"

"Miss Gudrun gave it to me before she left for Africa last week. She said I might need it if we were heading into the Oregon mountains this time of year. She didn't want me to get stuck in a storm with a hungry vampire."

"She's a wise woman, Terry," chuckled Ella, "and she likes you." He just blushed as she took a long swig from the bottle.

Kylie was grinning as she ordered room service for herself and Agent Sawchuk.

TWO DAYS LATER THEY were back in New York. They were picked up at the airport and driven directly into a rougher area of the sprawling city, to an office building with a warehouse attached at the back. Inside they passed the reception desk and went straight to the inner offices. A woman with a care worn face greeted them. "Everyone is waiting in the board room."

"Thanks you, Amanda, please join us," replied Ella, as she headed down the carpeted hallway. The others followed close behind.

"Greetings, my king." Ella smiled as she stepped through the door.

"Please be seated, people," replied the regal looking blond man with the wide shoulders. "Your message was a bit cryptic, Mother. Did you succeed?"

"We did, Harald, but I'm deeply concerned. The killer wasn't human, but neither was he one of our kind, as we had feared. Instead he was something I've not encountered before, but I believe Peter may have."

"Me? What do you mean, Mother?" The speaker was a short, heavy set fellow with a deep basso voice. That voice had a distinctly Russian accent.

"Ella. Please people, call me Ella. Yes, Peter. You once told me of a small tribe of people you encountered deep in the mountains of southern Russia. You said they were shapeshifters."

King Harald put his elbows on the table and leaned forward. "Shapeshifters? What kind of shapeshifters are we talking about? What did you find, Ella?"

"Perhaps it's better if we show you," said Kylie. "Tommy, can you put this video from my phone up onto the big screen?"

"Not a problem." The shy young man smiled as he accepted the phone from her hand and set to work. A moment later the huge screen leaped to life, and although the clip was a bit grainy, it was clear enough to follow. They all watched in silence until it was over.

As the screen went blank, Peter sighed deeply and leaned back in his chair. "Owan. I've not seen him for years. He was still a cub back then. Are you certain he's dead?"

"Can he revive as we do?"

"No, he cannot."

"Then he's dead, Peter," Ella replied kindly. "It was a long fall and he hit the ice then slipped beneath it. He didn't resurface."

"Someone must take word to his father. I guess that task falls to me."

"How do you know these people, Peter?" asked the king.

"Long ago, Sire, I was stalking a deer high in the mountains. I did not know a wolf pack was hunting too. We all charged at once. I had never seen another shapeshifter who wasn't one of us, and they hadn't seen any other except themselves. While we were looking each other over, the deer got up and ran away." Peter smiled and chuckled softly at the memory.

"Their leader stepped back and changed into a man, so I did also. They led me back to their camp and I spent several days learning to speak their language. It's very old and no other alive knows it, except their small band. They can also speak a dialect of Russian.

"Eventually we became friends, and I would visit them every few years or so. They're a shy people, preferring to stay hidden well back in their beloved mountains, never coming close to civilization.

"These aren't a savage people, Harald. I cannot imagine why he was here in America or why he so viciously killed those two young girls."

"Peter, what did he say to me?"

"He recognized who you are, Ella. I had told them many tales of the great cat who made me what I am. He said, 'Great Mother, protect my family.'"

Don't miss out!

Visit the website below and you can sign up to receive emails whenever Prudence MacLeod publishes a new book. There's no charge and no obligation.

https://books2read.com/r/B-A-ZKBBB-JTSWC

BOOKS 2 READ

Connecting independent readers to independent writers.

Also by Prudence MacLeod

Children of the Goddess
Lady Blue
Fallen Angel
Lady Justice
Lady Shadow
Lady Seeker
Watcher and Warrior
Shadow Ascending

Children of the Wild
Immortal Tigress

Forgotten Worlds
Suvi
Echo of the Past
Survivors
Ship
Fleet
Unite
IGEN

T.E.N.

Nova series
Novan Witch
Assassin of Nova
Beyond Nova
Claimstake
Red Nova

Watch for more at https://www.prudencemacleod.com/.

Telling a story is like knitting a sweater. Start with a ball of possibilities, pull out one small thread and begin. With luck and patience you will create something quite wonderful.

About the Author

On a far off windswept island Jennifer Crandall sits with her dogs and cats creating fantastic stories for all to enjoy. She publishes as JL Crandall, Prudence MacLeod, and Jenni Leigh.

Read more at https://www.prudencemacleod.com/.

www.ingramcontent.com/pod-product-compliance
Lightning Source LLC
Chambersburg PA
CBHW020954180626

46814CB00003B/1093

* 9 7 8 1 9 2 7 4 7 8 5 9 2 *